MELODY INTERRUPTED

J.R. TEASDALE

Pieeye Publishing Inc.
www.pieeyepublishing.com
Tel: 1-888-4pieeye (474-3393)
Fax: 1-888-421-9450

Here's pie in your eye!
Grab a piece while it's hot!

Copyright © 2003 by J.R. Teasdale.
All rights reserved. No part of this book may be reproduced or utilized in any form or by any means, electronic or mechanical, including photocopying, recording, or by any information storage or retrieval system, without permission in writing from the publisher.

Published by Pieeye Publishing Inc. with offices in Montreal, PQ. and in Plattsburgh, NY.

This novel is a work of fiction. Any references of events past or present or to existing people, living or dead, are purely concidental and intended only for the enjoyment of the reader. All names, characters, places and incidents are the product of the author's imagination and are used strictly fictitiously.

Book cover design by: Maxime Masse
Editing by: Laura Duke
Typesetting by: Pieeye Publishing Inc.

ISBN:0-9759435-1-0
Printed in USA

MELODY INTERRUPTED

I dedicate this romance to you
who have always known
that life's melody and harmony orchestrate
from love played by the human heart.

J.R Teasdale

Look for us online at:
www.pieeyepublishing.com

Reach us on line at:
1-888-4pieeye (474-3393)

Inquire about us:

Canada

43 Samson Blvd.
Suite 333
Laval, PQ H7X 3R8

USA

116 Consumer Square
Suite 333
Plattsburgh, NY 12901

Other books by J.R. Teasdale:

IMMEDIACY, suspense visionary with a metaphysical twist.

OCEAN TIDINGS, gripping romantic adventure.

MELODY INTERRUPTED

CHAPTER ONE

Deep within the entrails of Lincoln Center, through the corridors adjunct to Avery Fisher Hall, there wafted the spellbinding cries of a basso continuo—a sweet melancholic twang from the strings of a cello soloist.

Walking in that direction, Mark Spinner kept an ear pealed for the hypnotic chords of the baroque era—though he couldn't quite put a name to the composer.

He clipped a fast pace as he zigzagged a path along the corridor, jostling round handles of closed doors—to the right, to the left—listening intently in an effort to pinpoint the source of the music before reaching his destination.

When he pushed open Professor Minsk's door the melody deepened. Stepping through the doorway, he exhaled deeply and smiled with satisfaction when he spotted the cellist through the glass partition of the next room.

"Mark, is that you?" a gruff brusque voice demanded to know.

"Yes," he answered simply. He walked slowly and deliberately toward the glass as enthralled with the beauty of the cellist as he was with the piece she was playing.

She held the instrument gracefully between legs clad in black flared pants. A thick sweep of chestnut hair with shimmers of blond highlights fell below her shoulders, with the slightest of wave caressing her jaw line.

He could not see her eyes. She leaned her head toward her bow, her cheek almost caressing the stem of the instrument. He knew right away, she had to be a looker who believed in keeping fit, as the short bustier she wore molded her perfectly and revealed her bare arms and shoulders to be slim and sculptured.

"Who's the diva?" Mark asked, still mesmerized by the graceful movements. "And who is that composer? He sounds so familiar."

"You shame me!" The old man threw him a mock scowl. "You call yourself an agent? You peddle your sheet music and you don't know the composer of this masterpiece, or who this ethereal creature is? Better not let your clients know of your lapse." The rotund white-haired professor snickered and poked him good-humoredly.

"Aren't you going to tell me?" Mark was becoming impatient. He saw the young woman fold her sheet music and prepare to store her instrument.

"The composer...no. You'll have to find yourself. The cellist is Sarah Miller..."

"The Sarah Miller! The darling protégée of the Chamber Music Society?" Mark was shocked. "How do you know her? And what's she doing here in the gully of freshmen trenches?"

Bella, Frank Minsk's wife, assistant and den mother to many first-year students, answered for him. "She had an accident four months ago. She is recuperating under Frank's expert tutelage," smiling at her husband as she stressed the compliment. "She needs to strengthen her wrist with beginner's exercises."

"What kind of accident?"

"She was struck by..."

"Bella!" Frank clucked his disapproval. "This is personal to Miss Miller."

Bella nodded, remorse in her eyes. "You are right. I am sorry, Mark. You will have to ask Miss Miller herself," she edged with a smile. "You can ask her now." The old woman winked. "Here she comes."

Mark threw Bella a wry look. Yeah, right! He got the message. Anything too awkward to ask directly was probably worth the wait—maybe the permanent kind. "Never mind. It'll keep."

Sarah entered the antechamber, surprised to see the three of them seemingly waiting for her. Professor Minsk and his wife Bella she could understand. They were patiently waiting to close and lock-up these few rooms. This other gentlemen though, she didn't have a clue as to why he was there. She extended her hand and introduced herself.

"Pleased to meet you." Mark took her hand. "I'm Mark Spinner and I've heard a lot about you, Miss Miller," he cooed as he kissed the slender hand she placed in his.

"Have you? From the Professor and his wife?"

He shook his head caught in the snare of wide ocean-green eyes. She had to be the prettiest, most delicate..."Your reputation precedes you, Miss Miller. You're already famous... Antonin Dvorak, right?"

And when she smiled, full lips traced a sensuous edge over pearly white teeth. "Yes!" she exclaimed, surprised that he knew the composer of the piece she had been playing. "The Symphony in E Minor, or From the New World as they call it." She afforded this young man a second look. He was charming, she thought. Barely a couple of inches taller than she was, Sarah was able to perform an eye-to-eye scrutiny that revealed dark-fringed hazel eyes properly distanced from his nose and lodged below a wide forehead. In essence, his face reminded her of those of the leading men of the '30s. Especially as his dark-brown hair was thick and wavy. Had it not been for a thin hairline over his full upper lip, she might have mistaken him for a drama student, someone much younger than the years suggested by the confident gaze.

They were still facing each other, smiling, when Frank cleared his throat to attract Sarah's attention.

"Oh! Yes. I'm sorry, Professor Minsk. I left it." She pointed toward her case in the other room. "I won't be playing again this week. My wrist is a little painful. Can you do your usual magic?"

Mark looked at the pair of them questioningly.

Sarah laughed. "It's a disappearing act—the magic..." she added quickly as an explanation. "Professor Minsk is kind enough to store my cello out of view. It's easier for me, and the instrument is priceless. It was my mother's..." Her voice trailed off, as if she had revealed too much.

Mark nodded politely, unable to look away, like an automaton under a spell. Then, albeit reluctantly, he reverted his attention to Frank and Bella. He noticed the twinkle in Bella's eyes and the complicit grin she threw the pair of them—an endearing smile that called attention to little white whiskers protruding under her chin.

"Aunt Bella, you're a pip. Do you know that?" Mark kissed her on the cheek.

"And you are a dear boy," she nodded, stroking his face.

"They're your family..." Sarah was surprised. "No wonder you know the composers. You're a musician."

"He is not a musician." They heard Frank's gruff tone emphasized with a sweep of his arms. "Just a music peddler—he gives advice to budding musicians and sometimes acts as their agent."

"Thank you for the plug, Uncle Frank; but next time...

don't mention it…please."

Sarah laughed at Mark's comical match of words and sour facial expression.

"By the way," Mark pulled out an envelope from his coat pocket, "I need you to review this. I think it has potential."

"See what I mean?" scoffed Frank, rolling his eyes. "I give the opinion. He is just a voice box. He repeats my words to them."

"Oh, but you are such a wise man, Professor," Sarah answered, coming to Mark's rescue. "Seeking your opinion can only be to his credit." She looked up at Mark and smiled.

He acknowledged her kindness with a small head-bow. "I didn't come to trade niceties with you, Uncle." He patted the old man on the shoulder. "It's Brad's birthday on Saturday, and Julian asked me to invite you both for supper, and to bring gifts, of course." He extracted another piece of paper from his pocket. "This is a list of what Brad might like." He handed the paper to his aunt. "Anything on this list, Aunt Bella, will earn you first place on Brad's popularity chart."

"You are top on my popular chart," she told him with a smile. She glanced at the list. "We'll see," she answered.

"So, will you guys be there?"

"You know we will," said Frank. "And we shall come bearing gifts."

Mark nodded. Then with a sudden idea, he turned toward Sarah. "Want to come?"

She hesitated. Was he serious or just being polite?

"We would love to have someone famous in our little house, and you won't even have to regale us with any music. It'll just be social…"

Still she edged. Was Brad his son? Was this man married? Had she mistaken friendliness for flirting? She nodded her assent. What else did she have to do? "Yes, it would be nice." She turned toward Frank. "Should I come here first, we could go together?"

"Don't worry about that," answered Bella, looping her arm through Sarah's. "Frank and I will pick you up at your apartment. There is no need to come traipsing here on a Saturday afternoon."

As Sarah tottered away, hampered by the proximity of Bella's short stout frame, the older woman's pudgy arm wrapped tightly around her tiny waist, she could feel Mark's presence directly behind her. She turned to answer Bella, and was intimately aware through the corner of one eye that he was staring at her—ogling her, was probably a better rendition. So close was he, that to turn abruptly would have brought her face to face with his clean-shaven Calvin Klein-smelling cheek.

She scolded herself trying to rein her id back in check. Barely aware of Bella's exuberance as she chatted about her new class of students, or some other topic of conversation, Sarah walked beside her without uttering a word—a cloistered silence due in part to the mental replay of the piece she had just executed, and to the handsome stranger's troublesome presence lurking behind her. The soft scope of energy that emanated from Mark shrieked louder than any words Bella spoke directly next to her ear.

Presently Bella tugged at her arm while an inquisitive smile tilted her jovial face, eliciting a response from her—to a question—what question? Oh, God! she panicked, she hadn't heard the question. This was embarrassing, this girlish daydreaming about a stranger, a behavior she had always found ridiculous in other females, one that was having her flounder for a quick answer. What if Bella noticed...worse, what if Mark sensed her nervousness?

"I wouldn't bother with it, Sarah," Mark answered.

Bother with what! She couldn't ask Bella to repeat the question, not at this late stage in the conversation.

Mark said, "Brad will be happy with anything you give him. He's not even expecting a gift from you, remember?"

"So it's settled then," continued Bella. "I will shop for you and he'll never know the difference."

Sarah nodded, breathing such relief that she vowed not to give Mark another thought—at least not today, she smiled—not until she knew more about him. The abstinence would be proper penance for being such a ditz. But when he placed a hand delicately on her bare shoulder, her heart nearly leapt out of her chest.

"Can I drop you anywhere?"

Take a hold of yourself, girl. "No. Thank you. I have

errands to run."

Her tone brooked no coaxing. It was prim, proper and extremely polite. She noticed, on the other hand, that he was not intrigued by her sudden retreat—did not seem to faze him as he took his leave of both of them.

So their exchange had been one-sided after all, she realized, needled by a little pang of regret as she watched him walk away. She had lent his demeanor imaginary substance. At least she had been quick to realize it. No harm done, she decided. She also decided that his indifference would make the whole episode easier to forego.

"Tell your husband I will see him on Thursday. Tomorrow I have exams." Sarah smiled. "Wish me luck."

"You have no need for luck. You are very smart," smiled Bella. "And your French is impeccable. I know you will do well."

But alone in her apartment, a one bedroom third-floor walkup, Sarah found the Mark matter extremely difficult to let go. It was not so much that he was charming, or that he didn't seem to care where he pointed that cupid arrow of his. No. Her disappointment stemmed from the fact that, she had concocted this whole seduction scene, invented it, using nothing other than a fertile imagination. She was an artist, a little voice in her condoned. Nevertheless, loneliness was the wretched culprit, the wheeler-dealer responsible for this lapse into neediness. There was the difficult admission for her. She had always prided herself in being the symbol of independence, a liberated woman by the best of standards. Of course, growing up without parents while raised by nannies and lawyers probably had something to do with that desire to fend for herself.

But blame-game aside, orphaned or not, the loneliness she felt she knew she self-fabricated to erect privacy walls and avoid most social excursions. And though its weight was poignant at times, she relished its seclusion she paralleled to the need to be true to herself, to enjoy life the way she deemed was worth enjoying.

She stared at the horde of traffic down on Second Avenue, near the corner of 92nd Street. Central Park reposed a couple of blocks to the west, and the high-rises across the street obstructed her view of the sunset. There was no balcony from her living room window, and the small space she inhabited was devoid of sunlight for most of the day. But it was home. The 600 plus square feet furnished with olios and curios and a mish-mash of frippery was hers and hers alone. She did not have to share it with anyone. How lucky was that, she sighed.

The following Saturday was sunny but crisp, with temperatures hovering in the low sixties. Sarah had noticed the brisk drop in temperature when she had stepped up her morning stroll to the local gym to a fast jog, and the sweat on her brow had quickly cooled.

Now, three hours later—thanking God the clock on the wall was fast—she was late and still could not decide what to do with her hair. She had left it loose. Freshly washed, it was soft and manageable. The top layer fell nicely to curve her face, and the other layers dropped a few inches below her shoulders.

Bella had suggested she wear pants and a sporty top. This was a child's party and the planned fare was a cookout on the grill. You could not have more casual than hot-dogs and hamburgers.

Her doorbell rang and she acknowledged through the intercom. At the last minute, she grabbed a ribbon from the front drawer of the hall table and tied her hair in a loose ponytail, low on the nape of her neck.

This was better, she thought, as she surveyed her knee-length jeans frayed at the hem, her yellow stretchy tank top and a sweater for later, she knotted around her waist. For mid-May, the nights were still unseasonably cool.

She flew down the three flights of stairs and met Bella at the front door.

"I've kept you waiting; I'm sorry. Are you double parked?" she asked, slightly winded.

"The cabby doesn't mind. His meter happily clicks away." Bella laughed at the surprise on Sarah's face as she stepped onto the sidewalk to find a waiting taxi. Delicately the older woman stepped up to plant a kiss on Sarah's cheek. "You didn't think my husband still drove, did you?"

Sarah shrugged. "I guess I did. When you mentioned you would pick me up…I could have taken a taxi myself."

"Don't be silly," Bella told her as she slid in beside Sarah onto the back seat of the car. "Tell her, Frank. Tell Sarah how this is so convenient."

He turned in the front seat and winked at her. "Sarah, I would like you to meet a very dear friend of ours, Jeff Chandra. He's been driving us around for ten years. We try to ask for him whenever we can. He is an excellent driver."

"I'm pleased to meet you…"

"I am just Jeff." He smiled and handed Sarah a business card. "This is my direct telephone. If you ever need me to drive, you just call, I come running." He gave her an ear-splitting grin before putting the car in gear and driving away—tires screeching.

A thick white turban covered 'just Jeff's' head and a full facial beard hid his features. But when Sarah slipped his card into her handbag, her eyes met with dark friendly ones in the rearview mirror, and she had the keen sense that his kindness was genuine.

The ride to Long Island was comfortable and made enjoyable by conversation spiced with anecdotes from Bella and Frank's earlier years. It was easy to discern that they had been together a long time just by how well they meshed, and how each appeared unrehearsed in their respective roles—knowing where to end each other's sentences, where to add a detail or two.

So when the taxi drove up a flagstone driveway, she was surprised to find how quickly they had driven from the heart of Manhattan to the luxurious reaches of one of Long Island's trendier neighborhoods. Alighting, she stretched and took a deep breath of air, surveying her new surroundings.

She wondered if Mark lived here. If he did, he owned a gorgeous home. It looked more like a castle with its two gable roofs and mini turrets on each side. The two-story façade displayed beige and grey fieldstone halfway up the structure, while tan wooden slats covered the rest of the walls. The roof, pasted in slate-colored shingles, matched the stone's color perfectly. Borders of well-manicured shrubs of varied foliage ran several rows deep below white wood-framed windows. Sarah paused to take in the breadth and beauty of the front lawns stretching from each side of the circular drive. To the right, four Dogwood trees gorged with pink clouds of blossoms celebrated spring's arrival, and to the left, just as symmetrically positioned, four Bradford pear trees extended their silver blooms, a phosphorescent glow that contrasted nicely with their slender dark stems. If the property out back was as large as this, she figured the lot might be equivalent to one full acre.

Frank paid Jeff, who insisted on helping them unload the parcels from the trunk.

Sarah took the three bags Bella handed her. "These are your presents to little Brad," Bella told her. "There is also a little something in there for Julian." She smiled and tried to foster conspiracy with the quick motion of her thick grey brows. "Julian is a big baby when it comes to occasions like these. He does like his little toys."

Who was Julian, Sarah wondered. Why the need to humor him with a gift? Was he an older brother to Brad?

"Julian?" she inquired.

"Julian," resounded Frank Minsk. "He's Mark's older brother. This is his house. You'll meet him soon enough." Shadowing his eyes from the western sun with his hand, he looked toward the house and added, "Here he comes now."

To Sarah, Frank's remark sounded ominous. When she turned to look in that direction, she saw why. There was a wall of a man coming toward them, carrying a small child on his back as if he were no more than a weightless shoulder bag. If this was Mark's brother, she thought, they looked nothing alike. He was at least three inches taller, his head completely bald, and double Mark's shoulder breadth.

As he came closer, she noticed that the white sleeveless tank top he wore seemed stretched at the seams, ready to split. Sighing, Sarah conceded that only one of his arms had to be larger than the span of her thighs. Unable to look away, she noticed the dragon tattooed on the flexed, bulging right arm.

Gently he laid the boy down on the ground. He looked in her direction but barely acknowledged her as he greeted Frank and Bella with effusion. He shook Jeff's hand, and as he did, Sarah saw him place what looked like folded bills in the tall turbaned man's palm.

She had time to think, if he was not polite at least he was generous, before she felt her jeans being tugged at the knees. The little boy, having quickly gone from one hug to the next, was looking up at her with curiosity.

"You must be Brad." Sarah smiled as she looked down at the small face with the big dark eyes. He had a full head of tangled, tousled black hair and the eyes to match.

"And that's my dad," he pointed to the man who now gave her his undivided attention.

It was unavoidable; Sarah had to look at the man who had chosen to ignore her. As she did, she saw the resemblance to Brad in the eyes, except that Julian's were bigger, and of a peculiar color as if flecked with scintillating pieces of onyx that had just caught a light. They were certainly piercing, she sighed, and unyielding when honing in on their target.

She felt a little uncomfortable as she held out her hand. "Hello, I'm Sarah Miller—a friend of..." Sarah fleetingly glanced toward Frank and Bella, and as she did, the older woman leapt to her aid.

"She's an old friend of your uncle and mine," she beamed.

Yeah right, Aunt Bella. Thanks for the fix-up. I don't need your help in that department.

Sarah let her hand drop by her side. It was clear that this man was not going to reciprocate. He seemed to be going out of his way to be rude—for some reason known only to him, she rued.

He nodded with a slight grunt and proceeded to take the bags from his aunt and uncle's hands.

"Is this a gift for me?" young Brad asked her.

"Yes it is," she smiled tremulously, not understanding why no one was demanding that this man be at least civil to her. "How old are you today?" She turned her attention to the child who was adorable.

"I am five years old—a whole hand. This one," he added, showing his right one. "This is my right hand. The other one will have to wait until I am ten," he announced seriously.

Sarah bit back an attack of laughter, but it shone in her eyes as she glanced at Bella. The older woman gave her a hug. One thing was certain; this child was as sweet and precocious as a nursery rhyme character, thought Sarah; and she smoothed down the little boy's hair.

You can make goo-goo eyes at my son all you want. That's not going to score you any points with me. Without looking back, Julian wiggled his hand as a signal for Brad to walk with him. Obediently little Brad ran to catch up to his father, sliding his little hand into what resembled a giant mitt.

Glancing quickly at Frank, Sarah noticed that he was engaged in a subdued conversation with Julian as they walked a few feet in front of them. The old professor's demeanor with Julian was diametrically opposed to the good-humored banter he had shared with Mark the other day. She wondered if the earlier remark she had found ominous was Frank's way of warning her to traipse lightly around this one. She could well imagine the temper Julian must be capable of wielding. He carried the quarrelsome aura around him like a cloak. Nevertheless, she decided she would wait before casting a final ballot. Thinking it was only fair to do so, she wondered where Mark could possibly be.

"Mrs. Minsk..." Sarah began.

"Don't you think it is time you called me Bella?" She smiled. "If you don't, Julian is never going to believe that we are friends."

"You seem very concerned about what Julian believes...Bella," Sarah spoke tentatively, not really expecting an answer.

"He has had a difficult life," Bella whispered. Holding Sarah's hand, she continued. "My older sister Gertrude married Sam Spinner. It almost seems like several lifetimes ago... now. She is dead, you know. So is her husband, Sam. But they were extremely happy together. Everyone envied their love—especially me. Not that I was jealous, no. I was too young. You see, she was the eldest, and I was five years old when she married. I was going to be just like her when I grew up. Then, as sometimes these things happen and no one knows why, life only gave them one son. And they spoiled him. They spoiled Monty rotten. Whatever was not instant gratification, Montgomery Spinner wanted nothing to do with it. Still, we all thought he had matured when he married Ann, and later, when Julian and Mark were born. But, we were soon proven wrong. Monty gave up on his family when Julian was still in his teens. He took the inheritance his parents had left him when they died and never came back."

It was such a sad tale on so many levels. "Does anyone know where Monty is?"

Bella shrugged. "No. No one knows. As I was never blessed with children, we looked after the boys while Ann worked and earned a little money. Frank and I would help financially whenever we could. Then, when Julian was older, he began holding the reins for his family. Now his mother lives in Florida and wants for nothing. He takes care of Mark and his children; he's quite the business man."

"Where's the children's mother?"

"She left when Melissa was four—three years ago. Brad doesn't remember her, poor dear. The divorce papers were finalized last fall."

Sarah had her reservations about a woman who could pack up and leave her children behind. But a little voice told her Julian's acrid personality might well be the root cause. She could imagine how difficult it would be to pry the children away from this proud man.

Bella lowered her voice. "Frank would scold me if he knew I was telling you all this. He doesn't like it when I gossip…Anyway," she continued with an impish smile, "Julian was heartbroken. He loved Marissa very much. But she wanted to pursue a career in acting, so he gave her his blessing. She left for California with money he gave her, saying that she would be back twice a year to visit the children and that they could visit with her every summer. She never did. Even when he pleaded with her, threatened to cut her off, promised her money to come and visit the little ones. He even went to California last summer to be with her. The address she had left him was no longer valid. He was very angry. So he hired a private investigator to locate her and serve her with divorce papers."

"That must have been difficult on the children," Sarah acquiesced.

"It was, and is. Especially hard on little Melissa." Bella agreed.

This still doesn't give him a blank check to be rude to other women. She had done nothing to him, and certainly did not warrant suffering his contempt. She had had a difficult life as well, but she did not go around reminding everyone of this pathetic fact.

They heard Frank calling out to them.

Without realizing it, they had stopped walking, so engrossed were they in their conversation. Sarah waved to him, saying that they were coming promptly.

As they started for the front entrance, the loud honk of a horn behind them startled them. There was the answer to Sarah's question she had attempted to ask Bella five minutes prior.

Smooth and sleek, Mark's grey BMW Z4 convertible drove up and stopped barely one foot behind them.

She schooled herself to remain calm. This was a children's party and with what she had just learned about his brother Julian, she would do well to keep her feelings private. She would hate to have to simmer under that hot-tempered gaze.

"Ladies," he called out, jumping over the little roadster's closed door to walk toward them. "Wow," he interjected, taking in Sarah's attire. "Don't we look chic!"

Sarah smiled, comforted by his easy wit. This day already felt better—sunnier for sure. "I was warned that this was an outdoor meal with all the messy trimmings."

Bella nodded.

Mark was wearing cotton slacks and an open-collar green shirt. "And here I got all decked out for you," he told her, looking deep into her eyes.

Sarah didn't trust herself to add anything. Instead, she threw him a dubious look and laughed when he countered her disbelief with an exaggerated grimace.

Dutifully he kissed his aunt Bella on the cheek and scooped up both of them by the arm to march them toward the house.

From one of the windows in the formal living room, behind the pleats of lace curtains, Julian had quietly caught their little exchange. Frank was at the back of the house entertaining the children in the playroom. He was alone. There was no need to put on a face, to pretend, and a shadow crossed his eyes when he witnessed his brother's clownish behavior. There was only one reason Mark would act this way. Preening and prancing were an integral part of his mating ritual. And somehow Julian knew it wasn't Bella he was trying to impress.

They entered the house, laughing noisily and carrying on. Even Bella was enjoying herself, and it suddenly dawned on Julian that perhaps it was Mark his aunt was attempting to serve on a platter. Well good. Let his brother be the sacrificial lamb for once, the wistful thought crossed his mind.

Sarah stared at the imposing foyer and allowed her eyes to wander up to the twelve-foot ceilings, the circular oak staircase, and down to the two large rooms leading off each side of the main entrance. The floors were light oak—same as the balustrade—and the walls were a soft butter yellow. There were pastel colored vases on several decorative tall tables, depicting an array of vivid flowers. Natural light poured into the house and bathed in warm hues an exquisite arrangement of pale modern furniture and scattered rugs, and Sarah found herself reflecting how oddly paired were this house and its owner.

"This is breathtaking," she couldn't help saying to Mark who was watching her closely.

"Thank you," he said. "I'll give you the grand tour just as soon as I can locate that weird brother of mine."

"Give credit where it is due, Mark," Bella admonished. Turning her attention to Sarah, she added simply. "This house and all of its wonderful furnishings is Julian's handiwork."

"Not mine, Auntie," Julian answered as he entered the foyer. "More the hard work and good taste of a practical decorator."

"But you were the one who approved the decorator's choices," she added, opinionated and determined to give Julian the upper hand.

"Yeah, yeah. I see what you're doing," he told her with a rebellious frown. "Stop trying to pawn me off," he told his aunt while staring directly into Sarah's eyes. He had come closer—so close that she could see the ripple of tight muscles in his upper arms. Even the hardness of his chest was apparent through his thin cotton T-shirt.

The nerve of him, Sarah thought, trying desperately not to give in to anger. She stared back at him, wondering why he was not walking away. Why was he standing there, glued to the spot? She certainly was not going to back down first. Was he waiting for her to say something? As if such a lame comment deserved an answer. Who does he think he is? God's gift to women?

The long pause became awkward. She was aware of a child's voice calling out to Bella from somewhere and Mark offering the older woman his arm to take her there. She was left to fend for herself. When she refused to continue the stalemate and decidedly looked away—desperately pretending he was not addressing her, she attempted to move aside, to go around him. But he barred her only path of escape.

Taking advantage of the fact that they were alone, Julian flicked her face up with his hand—paw was a more fit description, she thought. Then his full mouth curled to one side as he gazed into her eyes. "This isn't what you and my aunt are attempting to do, is it?"

Ooh! Several sharp retorts came to mind. But she bit her tongue. First, she was a guest in this man's house; second, the thought of being a twig in the jaws-of-life grip of this man's arms was a humbling experience. Still, the fact that he was clearly barring her way against her will was tantamount to declaring war. She needed to post some kind of defense. "If I were you, Mr. Spinner, I would pick on someone my own size."

He laughed at her little girl words.

"As for your aunt playing matchmaker, where I am concerned you could never, ever be remotely mistaken for the intended party." Sarah aimed the sparks in her eyes to land in his. She knew by the loss of luster in his steel-grey ones that she had drawn first blood.

"Sarah! What's holding you up?" Mark wanted to know, already bored with the children's company. "What do you say we let Julian toil over his precious grill while we enjoy ourselves touring the rest of the house?"

"I would love that, Mark." Sarah shot Julian one last look. As she moved around him this time he let her go, the clenched fists by his side the only evidence of his frustration.

Mark led her around the bright airy corner to the left of the staircase. Four floor-to-ceiling window casings caught the eye and allowed the light of day to flow freely into the room. First, she noticed a sitting nook, more formal, with sofas and matching chairs. Then at the other end of the salon Sarah noticed the Steinway grand piano. On a side table next to it, lay a small flute and an oboe floating in mounds of sheet music. A metronome dangled precariously on the edge of a lounger's arm, and Sarah picked it up and placed it on the table beside the flute. The instruments seemed perched in readiness as though the band had struck a pause and they were poised for their return. Children's large picture books were strewn about the piano bench, and Sarah guessed that this room was not off-limits to Melissa and Brad.

"Listen, what was that between you and Julian back there—when I first arrived? I sensed a little tension…"

Sarah smiled, remaining poised and placid. "No tension. He just sort of wondered who I was—which is natural, you know, to want to know why I am here."

She didn't know Mark well enough to trust him with any other information. She certainly didn't relish being the instigator of any ill ease between Julian and the rest of his family. Anyway, that actually was what had spurred Julian's curiosity.

"Who plays the oboe?" Sarah asked.

"Julian. At least he tries. You can just imagine how strange he looks—this huge klutz blowing into this slim conical double-reed mouthpiece. I think the real contest is for his fingers to steer clear of the other holes—you know…when he's trying to poke one down…"

Mark imitated his fingers tripping over each other in an awkward manner, and his comical facial expression drew a smile from Sarah.

"You and your brother sure don't look alike, except perhaps for the mouth and the chin…and the bottom jaw line."

"Trust me," he said emphatically. "That is where the resemblance ends, I promise you." He gestured. "I told him you were coming. He just doesn't listen. He doesn't care about much of anything since he lost Marissa. He still loves her something fierce."

Sarah didn't want to tell him she knew the story, nor did she want to continue the conversation. "What's this room here?"

"This is the nanny's room. She arrives at 7:00 in the morning and leaves at 7:00 at night, so the room affords her a little privacy. Through that door, on the right, is a washroom that also serves as laundry room. And through here," he pointed out as he opened the door, "is Melissa and Brad's playroom."

As they entered, Bella and the children greeted them warmly.

"Where are the others?" asked Mark.

"They are outside, fiddling with the grill. Robert is giving them a hand."

"Who is Robert?" Sarah asked curiously.

"He is the gardener and fix-it man Julian employs," Bella answered with a smile.

"I am going to continue giving this lovely lady my undivided attention, show her the rest of our home, if you will excuse us."

"You go ahead, you dear boy," Bella told him.

Mark showed Sarah the dining room, the exercise room, and the butler's pantry, where a woman from Westbury village cooked up a storm three times a week to stock the cupboards and freezers. He displayed the many nooks and crannies, had her sample the window seat in the library, then marched her up to the second floor to see the other rooms.

"There is no need to show me everyone's sleeping quarters," Sarah protested. "I get the gist of the house's layout by now."

But the instant they reached the recesses of the upper corridor, Mark turned and pinned her against the wall, his kind hazel eyes transformed into dark green fiery liquid.

"I've wanted to do this ever since we met," he breathed, molding his body into hers. He sighed heavily, coming in closer. "This is so nice." The palms of his hands were flat against the wall behind her so that his arms barred her way.

"Mark," she protested. "Please." She pushed against him with all her might. But he was a heavy weight, difficult to budge.

"You want this too," he breathed. "I sensed it, that day at the conservatory."

She was angry for not being more forceful. But as he came closer, his hands traveled over her and she felt his arousal digging into her hip. Soon his heat became contagious. It inflamed her lower limbs to the point that she almost collapsed. She had not known intimacy with a man. She had only ever been the recipient of light kisses and lame caresses. Truth was, she was not particularly proud to be the world's oldest virgin. She was just as primed and ready as he was, maybe more. But not like this. She wanted her first time to be special. This was too fast.

A distant part of her brain raised a red flag. They were inches away from the door to his bedroom, and she knew that if he kept on sliding her toward the entrance as he was now, by inching her along the wall while continuing to bathe her neck in dozens of wet hungry kisses, once inside she would not be able to resist him. The thought of Bella and Frank and the children downstairs brought her back to her senses. But it was the sobering thought of Julian's wrath that gave her the courage to grind the heel of her shoe into his foot, causing him to recoil in pain just enough to give her the out to run to the top of the stairway.

There she paused, cheeks flushed and breathing heavily. She looked down at her jeans and realized that he had managed to unfasten them. This is not how she had envisaged her first intimate encounter with Mark Spinner.

She refastened her jeans, redid her ponytail and dared to look at where they had just been standing. He was leaning his back and head against the wall, looking straight ahead and refusing to glance in her direction.

"I thought you wanted this as much as I did," he told her roughly.

"I did. I mean, I do…just not so…"

Only then did he turn to look at her and walk over to where she stood. His motion practically had her running headlong down the stairs.

"Please," he stopped her with his hand on her arm. "Don't go. I'm sorry. I'm sorry if I rushed you. I don't normally do this with a woman—I can assure you."

"Maybe it's my fault," she attempted, her eyes locked with his.

He shook his head, a smile finally appeasing the torture on his face. "Don't blame yourself for my stupidity. I just hope we can…still be friends."

"For a minute, I thought you were going to say that you just hoped we could try again." She smiled, bolstered by the knowledge that they were precariously perched on the first step of a steep winding staircase.

Instead of affirming his intentions, he stroked her face gently and nodded. "Can we…try again?"

His humble question, this graceful capitulation after what she knew must be painful disappointment, drew her breath away. Had they been alone in the house, his attitude would have more than secured a complete about-turn from her.

"Yes," she whispered intently. "I'm counting on it."

He bent to kiss her lips, ever so gently, and a delicious shiver ran through her limbs. When he finally released her, she had to clasp the railing firmly to steady her steps and not lose her balance preceding him down the stairs.

CHAPTER TWO

They were late arrivals to the meal. Everyone was already seated around a long picnic table set with quite a spread, laid out very festively for the cookout.

Sarah finally got to see the yard. And as her eyes circled the space, she smiled to herself. She could have bet money. The property had to be close to an acre's worth of land.

Mark proudly pointed out the screened, oversized in-ground pool and deck, the Jacuzzi hidden under the trees, and delineated the rim of the property that was hedged with huge cedars.

It swept more like grounds, she decided. If there was a fence surrounding the property, it was well camouflaged behind a clever arrangement of bushes and trees.

She neared the end of the table where Bella and Frank sat. She was suddenly aware of Mark's arm around her shoulders and did not like what the possessive grasp implied. They had not been intimate inside the house and she hated giving everyone the impression that there was now something more than a casual relationship between them. She particularly did not care for the mocking glint she detected in Julian's eyes.

Distancing herself from Mark, she commented on the variety of succulent food laid out on the table.

"Mrs. Casey came in from Westbury yesterday and prepared these little confections and all the mouthwatering goodies you see." Bella supplied. "Here, Sarah, have a seat between Julian and me."

"Nonsense," Mark replied. "Come and sit over here beside me."

Bella's eyes were insistent, but it was Julian's eyeful dare that finally tossed her firmly between him and his aunt, trembling like the leaf between two pages when it knows the book will slam shut.

Frank introduced Melissa to her and Sarah liked her immediately. She resembled Mark more than she did Julian with her wide hazel eyes and easy smile. Even her long dark hair curling around a heart-shaped face was the same color as that of her uncle.

"There is smoked salmon," Julian told her in a more civil tone than she had previously heard, "if you don't like meat. There is potato salad, vegetable stir-fry, baked corn on the grill—help yourself."

Sarah dug in, just realizing how hungry she was, and

wondered how he knew she preferred fish to meat.

"It's too bad it's too early to go swimming, Julian," Frank said. "Sarah enjoys swimming—don't you, Sarah?"

"I do."

"Well, then," Julian told her between two mouthfuls. "We'll have to have you back…when it's warmer," he added with loads of undertone she did not hazard to guess.

She pondered, he was most likely making amends for his previous rude behavior, and decided to take it at face value—though it was late coming, she rued.

Half way through the meal, Julian told Robert to sit and eat with them. "You've done enough, my friend." Then, turning towards Sarah, he asked her directly. "So, what's your story?"

What was that about? "I beg your pardon?"

"How do you know my aunt and uncle?"

Bella gave her a wink and a small nod of encouragement.

"I play the cello," she said simply. "Your uncle is giving me…pointers."

He looked at her searchingly as she turned away, quickly averting her eyes. It was clear to Julian that she didn't want to talk about her predicament—whatever it was.

"A musician." He pronounced the word slowly. "Temperamental, moody, unreliable—that's what I've found most of them to be."

"You wouldn't say that about your uncle, would you?"

Bella asked him with a charming frown.

"I did say, most of them, Auntie. Most of them," he repeated staring at Sarah.

"I always find it's a mistake for the pot to call the kettle black, Mr. Spinner," she answered in dulcet tones.

He smiled. "Why? You can take a stab at me—go ahead. Most people do when they first meet me—you know." He flexed his arm and pointed to it, "big here," he pointed to his head, "small here," he simulated the beat of his heart by flitting his hand over his chest, "even smaller here. I'm used to it. Doesn't bother me."

"Then why bring it up?"

"You seemed embarrassed by what you do. I just thought I'd rid us both of the stereotypes—easier to talk."

She realized his outrageous assumption was to draw her out—get her angry enough to spill. She considered that if anything, his malicious way of extracting confidences was having the opposite effect. It made her feel trapped. How could she argue that she was proud of being a musician without explaining why she had shied away from giving him specific details about her affairs? How could she politely state that the private matter of her life was none of his business. How it was off-limits to a rude ditz like himself who would not understand what made her tick if he lived to be one thousand years old.

She took a deep breath, realizing with a smile that she had stereotyped him. She had cast him as a large oaf who suffered from the proverbial foot-in-the-mouth disease, incurably. But she had not judged him on his looks. On the contrary, she had taken her cue from his personality and his less than amenable demeanor.

She would have rather not supplied him with any answer. However, Bella, Mark, and Frank were waiting with their mouths open for some form of riposte from her.

"I don't believe in stereotypes," she finally said. "But I tend to agree with you. There exist many victims of typecasting. Although most of them—victims of circumstances, that is—can be players who've simply gotten caught up in their own game. Most of them..." she reiterated, staring at Julian.

Mark was in the process of taking a swig of beer. He barely had time to turn and spit it out to the side, so quickly did the laugh rise out of him. Frank put his hand over his mouth to hide the grin and Bella suddenly became engrossed with Brad playing with his food.

"Good one, Sarah," Mark told her, coming up for air.

When she dared catch a sidelong glance of Julian, she found an enigmatic smile hanging over his face while he continued eating, but said nothing.

"Brad loves the remote control jeep you got him, and thank you for the video game," Julian told Sarah gruffly. "It is okay for me to talk to you now—without having my head chewed off?"

They had already dished out and eaten the cake. Coffee, tea and cognac had replaced soda, wine and beer. The discarded melted candles attested to Brad's five years of age. The evening was winding down.

"I apologize if I was a bit crude during supper," Sarah admitted. "And even though you've been less than friendly ever since I got here, that was no excuse for my being rude. Oh, and your aunt picked out the toys."

"I sort of figured she had. The jeep was on the list I gave Mark. Speaking of Mark, why isn't he glued to your side?"

Once more, the tone was sarcastic. "He went to get me some Belgian white chocolate liqueur from the liquor cabinet. I had the unfortunate mishap of mentioning that I enjoyed it once, so he ran there to fetch it for me."

"Quite the Galahad, our Mark—wouldn't imagine this bothers you a whole lot?"

She bit back a retort she wanted to hurl at him. His conversation with her was nothing but one long sneer. She only needed to tolerate it one more hour at the most, she consoled herself. Mark had promised his aunt and uncle would be ready to leave soon.

"So, what kind of business do you do, Mr. Spinner?"

He laughed at the use of his surname. "Call me Julian and I'll tell you," he baited her.

All she had to do was not comply and she would be rid of him. "Does this mean that if I don't, you'll have nothing more to say to me?" She half expected him to laugh. Mark would have done so. In fact, coming back with two glasses and a bottle, he did.

"Boy, bro, my girl has your number. She knows how to cut you down to size."

She was his girl now, Julian thought as he rose, punishing anger lurking in his eyes.

That man has no sense of humor, Sarah told herself with a sigh. He is so full of his own importance. Yet, she could not help watching as he walked away, mesmerized.

Julian stopped suddenly, turned and added. "Oh, I forgot to tell you. You are my guest for the evening. Uncle Frank is not feeling well and Aunt Bella has asked if you'd be kind enough to stay in case she needs a hand, Sarah."

She had not expected the utterance of her name to sound so soft coming from his lips…But this was ridiculous. There were people here who could help Bella—why her? "I can't stay," she smiled. "I have work tomorrow."

"It's Sunday."

"I have to practice; besides, I have no change of… clothes."

"I have everything you'll need," he said with some finality as he turned from them to walk away. "Including clean underwear," he shouted before disappearing out of sight.

"Why is your brother so…so hateful to me? Did I do anything to displease him?"

"Don't mind him. He's turned into a big bad bear since Marissa left him. We all ignore his moods and bouts—as you probably noticed at supper. He's not a bad guy—just lonely, I guess."

"He has a funny way of seeking company."

"Life's dealt him a few blows. He wasn't always the successful business man he is now."

"What does he do?"

"He owns a couple of gyms downtown Manhattan—big ones—three of them, actually. And, he opened a couple of Karate dojos where he gives first-class instruction. He also dishes out free lessons to the needier kids. Uses the moves to get into their psyche and teach them a thing or two about life. He's surrounded himself with excellent instructors. It helps."

"Knowing this makes it even harder to understand why he acts the way he does." Sarah shook her head, more puzzled than if Mark had not confided in her.

"He blames himself for our father leaving. And don't ever tell him I said this. He'll hang my hide out to dry."

She shook her head, suddenly interested.

"He was in with the wrong crowd—Julian, I mean. Partying, smoking. By the time he was thirteen, he'd already graduated into heavier stuff—boosting cars, joy riding. It didn't help that he was so much taller and bigger than most guys his age. He just seemed to fit in better with the thugs. He was never school smart and kids used to make fun of him—call him noodle head and other pathetic, lamebrain names. Thugs and thieves made him feel as if he belonged, you know?"

She nodded.

"When our good-for-nothing father secretly left,

Julian thought it was because of his troubles with the law; but then my mother started relying on him more and more—best thing that ever happened to Julian. He got a couple of breaks, started using his body as an asset rather than a hindrance. Uncle Frank helped him start his first business venture…Still, he had to grow up in an awful hurry. That's why sometimes he still acts as if he's king of the hill. I let him. I figure what's the harm? He deserves it."

No wonder, she thought, they all humored him as much as they did. "What I said to him tonight must have been doubly hard for him and for the rest of you to hear," she admitted with a jab of guilt, remembering her less than kind words.

"Nah! Don't worry about it. He's got tough skin. The kind of skin that a lot of what we say just bounces off. He won't remember in the morning."

"I hope you're right."

"Speaking of morning, I have pajamas I can lend you—nice silk ones." His eyes were aglow as he spoke.

"I really don't think I can stay," Sarah said, wondering where she would sleep and if the bedroom doors had locks. She also knew that if she did not stay, the family might construe this as one more affront to Julian.

"How many bedrooms does this house have?"

"You should have allowed me to continue with my tour. You would know by now."

He was a rogue and he knew it, she conceded, shaking her head ruefully, but such a handsome one.

"There are six bedrooms and the same number of bathrooms. Two are guestrooms. Prepped and ready to serve. Their adjoining bathrooms are stocked with toothbrushes, toothpaste and all the other accoutrements you would find at the finer hotels."

"Was he serious when he said he had...accessories for me?"

"He must. Marissa had cupboards full of them, many still with price tags on them when she left." He became suddenly pensive. "I thought he'd given all that away to charity. At least that's what Aunt Bella once said...I don't know," he shrugged. "If Julian says he does, then he does."

"There is no guarantee it would fit me."

"Yes, it would. You and Marissa are pretty much the same size. She is shorter, is the only difference."

Sarah had no arguments left. One thing was certain; she would have to avoid the man in front of her. He leaned over to rest his right arm on his bent knee, his foot propped up on the bench not two inches from where she sat, while his other foot stood planted firmly on the other side of her feet. His posture reminded her of a cat sleek and coiled, ready to pounce.

She made a motion to indicate she wanted to move. He had to extricate himself for her to rise. "I guess I'd better go see if your aunt needs me."

Once indoors, Sarah noticed how quiet and empty the big house seemed, except for muted contemporary music in the background—transported throughout by some sort of speaker system.

Sarah called out to locate Bella. She heard a faint answer coming from one of the rooms, climbed up the stairs quickly and followed the sound to the third door on her right.

The door was ajar. Even so, she knocked lightly and obeyed the request to enter. The room resembled a small suite, furnished tastefully, showing a refrigerator in one corner, bookshelves and a writing desk on the opposite wall—there was even a computer on the writing desk.

Frank was lying in bed, clearly indisposed, and Bella was sitting by his side applying a compress to his forehead.

"Be a dear, Sarah, and help Julian with the children. Little Melissa wanted me to read to her. I can't. I don't dare leave Frank right now."

"What's wrong with the Professor?" Sarah asked concernedly as she stepped into the room.

"I am perfectly fine," he answered in short spurts of breath. "I just need to get my wind back."

"It's his heart," Bella supplied with a wan smile. "He just took a little pill. I want to monitor his signs for the next hour or so. Julian could use your help with Melissa."

"What about little Brad?" Sarah asked, worried about the professor.

Bella checked her watch. "It is 9:00. Brad has been asleep for almost an hour."

"I don't need anybody's help with my own children," Julian answered, his sudden appearance in the doorway dwarfing the room. "You just take care of Uncle Frank, I'll manage the rest." Before slipping out of sight, he threw Sarah an ominous look that dared her to interfere.

Bella hand-signaled her to come closer. "Don't listen to him," she whispered once Sarah had reached the foot of the bed. "He's too proud. Be a dear and go to Melissa. Her room is up the flight of stairs at the end of the hall."

"I hadn't realized there was a third floor," Sarah said.

"There isn't, not really. Julian had the huge attic converted into two rooms for the children and a little bathroom in the middle for them to share. Very pretty rooms, under the gables."

Sarah bent and gave Frank an encouraging smile as she rubbed Bella's back.

Bella winked at her giving her the nudge to go.

Sarah ran silently down the hall, hoping she would not encounter the big bad Julian, and quickly scaled the little winding staircase that led to the upstairs loft.

Once in the attic, she smiled at the pretty picture of a hallway tiled with plastic dinosaur scales. It led to a first door that looked like a bright, colorful candy cane. Etched on the door were the words Melissa's Dollhouse.

Down the hall, perpendicular to the first room, was a green door displaying the picture of a one-eyed pirate. She guessed that the second door led to Brad's room. *By now, the birthday boy must be sound asleep. In the middle must be the bathroom Bella mentioned.* But she saw no hall access to it.

Sarah rapped lightly on the pink door, then hearing Melissa's invitation to come in, turned the handle and entered.

"Hi!" Melissa said, surprised to see her. "Where is Aunt Bella?"

"She's helping your Uncle Frank. He's not feeling well." Sarah cast her eyes at the colorful children's furniture, the nursery rhyme characters—some stuffed, others in tapestry wall hangings—the middle beam that had been painted and decorated to resemble a candy cane stick, the lace curtains covering the windows under the gables, and sighed aloud. "Your room is charming, Melissa." The sloping ceiling each side of the high beam imparted the feeling of shelter and privacy.

"Thank you." The little girl smiled. "I was hoping my aunt could help me with some of this math.

"Do you want me to go and get your father instead?"

Melissa turned and looked at her squarely. She pursed her lips as if to say something, but refrained to do so, refocusing instead on the book in front of her.

Sarah suddenly remembered Mark's words about Julian's scholastic difficulties. How could she have forgotten. She rued her stupidity. It made more sense now, Julian professing he didn't need help with his children, and Bella whispering that he was too proud. But then again, how difficult could second-grade math be?

"Maybe I can help you with it," Sarah offered gently.

"That would be nice." Melissa moved over on the bench she was using at her desk.

Sarah sat beside her and read some of the problems—twice, to better get the gist—and had to recognize that the math was very advanced for a seven-year-old. "What grade are you in?"

Melissa shrugged. "I don't know. My teacher says that this is secondary one mathematics curriculum. I'm not to study it, just familiarize myself with the logic."

Sarah was stunned. "How many grades have you skipped?"

"None. I study at home—so does my brother. The teachers come here. We have four of them."

Sarah slumped with the news and would have loved back support at that moment. How well she remembered feeling what Melissa was experiencing. As a child she had endured the same anxieties. Alone, never allowed to study with other children her age, a procession of teachers coming and going freely while she was a prisoner of imaginary, pink-colored walls. She remembered the struggle to comprehend, the desire to please—to keep the movement forward, while never knowing when or if it was ever going to end. She had fancied that once she knew everything there was to know, they would have to allow her to leave her gilded cage—take flight and do as she pleased.

"Is everything all right, Sarah?"

Sarah smiled. "Sure, sweetie, let's see if we can't do some of these problems."

"There you are!" Mark trumpeted from the doorway. He hadn't knocked or made his presence heard, and Sarah couldn't help thinking how asking Melissa's permission before entering was only polite.

"Here I am, yes. And you, kind sir, ought to ask a lady's permission before entering her private boudoir," Sarah told him with a smile. She peered at Melissa's wide assenting grin and knew she had pleased her no end.

"But this is not a boudoir. It clearly states on the door that the premises are a doll's house."

"The more reason to tread lightly, sir." Sarah mocked.

"I agree with Sarah," Melissa added excitedly, jumping on the opportunity to be heard. And Sarah thought her a most precocious little girl.

"Okay! Everybody out," a loud stern voice announced behind them.

"But, Daddy, Sarah is helping me with my math problems."

Sarah inhaled sharply as Julian's eyes stared into hers, as sharp as razor-edged daggers. Sarah's first urge was to duck for cover. Instead she rose, smiled at Melissa, and promised they would look at them in the morning after breakfast.

Slipping by Julian, she jumped when she heard him

mumble though clenched teeth. "Don't make promises you can't keep."

Mark had inched out of the room, and when she met with him on the second floor stoop he brandished a pair of pajamas. Only then did Sarah allow herself a long drawn out breath. She glanced behind her and thanked God she wasn't followed.

Mark laughed, guessing at the panic on her face. Then dismissing the matter entirely, he handed her a neatly folded bundle. "One pair of silk PJs for my lady, as promised."

"Thank you. Now if you'll tell me where my room is, I shall retreat for the night and reclaim some sanity," she stated to stay in character. It was better to play and pretend than to focus too much on the charming man handing over her nightwear.

He indicated the second door down the hall, on the other side of the staircase. "I'd walk you over myself," he smiled. "But I think you've been frightened enough for one day."

That was a mouthful; she nodded as she bade him goodnight with a peck on the cheek.

Finally enclosed in the privacy of four walls, she breathed a long sigh of relief. She noticed the latch on the door and locked it feeling so much better knowing she would not be disturbed.

Mark had not exaggerated about the supplies in the large adjoining bathroom. There was even a hair dryer and an electric massage pad. But ferret as she might, she found nothing she could wear in the morning.

She took a long soothing shower, yet she could not rinse away the day's strange sensations. The attraction she harbored for Mark was so potent. It almost matched curve for curve the repulsion she felt for Julian. She loathed the man's arrogance, despised his smugness. She pitied his small children whom she figured had to placate his every whim. She shivered with this last thought as she towel-dried her hair and slipped into the pajamas Mark had given her.

When she padded barefoot into the bedroom, she jumped, barely managing to stifle a piercing scream.

There stood Julian, waiting for her to emerge from the bathroom, it seemed. He wore knee-length brushed cotton pants resting on his hips, and a short matching kimono, loose fitting and untied, displaying a rock-hard torso and a washboard stomach.

He gave her a wicked smile when he noticed the fear that stubbornly would not subside from her eyes.

"What are you doing here," she stammered, out of breath as if she had just run an up-hill marathon. She had locked the door. She knew she had. Had she taken the wrong room? Were these his quarters? That was the only explanation, she decided, struggling to regain her composure.

"I came through the connecting door." He indicated with the tilt of his head the door beside the night table she had not noticed before.

"You have a connecting door from the master suite to

the guest room?"

"This used to be the children's room. When they were babies it was easier to get to them in a hurry...I knocked, but didn't hear anything. I thought you might still be out with Mark. I was going to put a few clothes on the bed for you when I heard you coming out of the bathroom."

That made sense. She let go a sigh, removing the towel from her damp hair so that it fell about her, long and limp.

The tigress transformed, he thought, transfixed to the spot beside the bed, unable to stop staring at her. "I see Mark loaned you PJs." He tried to smile to relieve some of the tension. "Well," he added when she wouldn't answer, "since you're here, you should come across to rummage for something to wear. You'll be better able to choose what fits and what doesn't."

That also made sense. She followed him across to the other room which he had decorated in the same dark rich tones. The only variance was the wallpapers and picture frames. His walls were covered with a geometric design and adorned with photos of fast cars and soft-looking women; hers were done with a floral print and paintings of landscapes and cities.

He brought her to the closet nearest to the bed and she saw lingerie displayed on the shelves and a number of outfits still hanging on the rod.

"I've been meaning to have it cleaned out—I just haven't had the time."

Sarah picked up a bra and fit her hand inside to span the cup, trying to size it. She noticed him staring at her intently, so she turned her back to him. The panties were easy to fit as they still had tags on them; and as she checked the outfits, she wished he was not hovering behind her, breathing down her neck.

"Aren't you going to try them on?"

Was he crazy? Did he think she was going to strip in front of him to parade in his ex-wife's underwear?

"In the bathroom," he added, clearly laughing at her. "Alone," he continued when his jab received no response.

"That's a no," she told him, overly prim. Sarah looked at him with disgust on her face. Tired and edgy, unused to this much tyranny in one day, she needlessly added. "This Vin Diesel look you're trying to mimic might hold power over some women, but not over me." Her words were not yet totally out before she knew she had made a mistake. They sounded horrible, even to her, disgruntled as she was. But mostly she detected the error of her words when she sensed how coiled and tightly wound they drove him to be. So preoccupied had she been with her own feelings, she had never noticed the warning light in his eyes illuminating his whole body as a danger zone.

He came closer, turning her around to face those glaring onyx eyes.

Maybe if she apologized and pleaded with him that she had been joking...She had crossed the line and she knew it.

"Since you are so fond of stereotyping me, why not guess at the kind of delicious game I am about to engage, and am likely to get so caught up in...I am going to push and push and forget that I am merely playing?"

Her legs went weak at the knees.

He spoke his threat in soft menacing tones.

As he clasped her shoulders she felt her heart pounding all the way up in her throat. Her situation was a precarious one. She had to do something. But what? There was no one likely to come to her rescue. Everyone had retired for the evening, tucked away behind closed doors. Some teeny voice of reason told her it was way past the time to reason with him. If she screamed, someone might hear her. Even if no one did, it might bring him back to his senses.

But when she tried, he interpreted her gesture correctly and like lightening clamped down hard on her mouth, choking the sound out of her with his tongue lodged at the back of her throat.

She tried to kick him but her feet seemed wedged in cement, squeezed between his own. He strapped his huge left arm against her back, while his hand held her right shoulder from inching in the slightest direction and his shoulder blocked her right arm from moving. This left his left hand free to move and do whatever it pleased, and roam it did.

She was furious. And even as tears of humiliation and frustration brushed her cheeks, she was determined to report him in the morning. Who did he think he was? What gave him the right? Did he think that because he was adept at undoing her top and caressing her bare back she was going to unhinge and give in? Even if her nipples became rock-hard from his constant caresses, it didn't mean that she was surrendering.

She had to open her mouth as wide as she could—just to breathe; his mouth was seared to hers and his tongue took up all her air space. But it was when he pulled down her pajama pants to a little heap on the floor that she became angrier than ever. There was no way her innocent taunting deserved this amount of white ravishing rage.

Angrily, she instigated her own line of attack by pushing his tongue back into his mouth, as far back as she could. She was actually surprised how easy it was to do this. When she kept his in check by shoving hers at the back of his throat, she felt him shake and heard him moan. That's when he picked her up and brought her to the bed.

He deposited her trembling body on top of the soft coverlet, lying down on top of her while supporting his weight. But looking down into her eyes, he suddenly retreated.

She dropped back onto the pillows. Her mouth was throbbing, probably swollen, she thought. She put a hand to her lips and felt them tender. Was he gloating? Is that why he had stopped—to brazenly gaze at her from head to toe, taking in every curve of her body with hungry eyes?

"It still isn't too late to stop this," he whispered hoarsely.

The nerve of him! She had wanted to stop all along.

Is this what winning meant to him? The need to prove to her that he could play without getting caught up in the game?

Well, she was in charge now. He was pleading with her. It was her turn to make him dance and forget whom he was....Of course, she would show him she was not some little girl who could not fend for herself.

She arched her body to touch his.

Still he did not budge. His eyes bore into hers, and suddenly they were angry. Sarah realized he was poised to get up and leave her.

At once, she began caressing his lips with her fingers. She moved her hands down to his chest—down still, until he stopped her, cursing at her as he did.

"You little witch!" he spat. "Keep this up and you're going to feel it in the morning."

As he made the motion to rise and leave, she held on to his leg. "Seems to me you are the one who's running scared. Why? No follow-through?" she taunted him, her breath coming out in short spurts. She just had to win.

That was the last thing Sarah remembered thinking, hearing or saying. The unleashed passion in the hours that followed served only to fuse their bodies and minds into one blazing torch. She lost track of time. All she remembered was that every time Julian doused their flame with a stream of satisfaction, the fires would ignite moments later, like hot lava spewing through burning ashes, over and over again, until spent and exhausted, she slipped into oblivion.

Sarah woke up the next morning in the guest room. It was past 9:00, and she felt lost and disoriented, as groggy as she looked.

As bits and pieces of the previous night began surfacing, she wondered if she had not dreamt the whole episode. She stood to go to the washroom and the pain racking her lower limbs brought reality to the forefront. Every bone in her body felt as if it had been crushed, especially her legs. The nightmare was real.

She gazed at her pale swollen face, at the lack-luster reddened eyes and panicked. She had no make-up with her. Her only hope was soaking her face in cold water to try to bring some color back into it.

She sat on the bed eyeing the clothes she had picked out for today and detested them on sight. Julian must have brought them when he carried her back to the guestroom, in the early hours of the morning. She had been so passed out, she had not even noticed.

One thing was painfully true. Julian was right when he had said that she would feel it in the morning. But the worst pain was not the physical kind. Knowing she had egged him to continue when he had wanted to stop was by far the worse humiliation.

Oh, sure! The night before, her stint had felt akin to power and vengeful manipulation. Today, it just seemed utterly stupid. She could not believe she had talked herself into thinking that she was giving in to him for spite. She was no better than some drunk who found reasons to condone his next binge. Her sense of right and wrong had severely betrayed her last night. Never in her wildest machinations could she have imagined sex to be so overpowering and all-consuming. She had been engaged for eight months. What was so different between Julian and Serge—her former fiancée—to warrant this total abandonment of all rules and precautions? She couldn't even remember if he had worn protection. One important distinction was that she loathed Julian with all the comprehension of the word's subtleties she could muster. She would look up more meanings in the thesaurus later; for now, she would find a way to leave this house without attracting everyone's attention to her predicament, and never see this man again, or hope to die.

She got dressed in yesterday's fare while devising a plan to leave quietly, without having to bid farewells to everyone concerned—especially to the master of the house. Then she remembered her promise to little Melissa and she cringed. She also remembered Julian's words, about meeting up with difficulties with keeping her promise, and wondered if he had not planned this all along. She was losing it, becoming hysterical. She scolded herself to remain calm.

She heard a knock at the door.

"Who is it?" Sarah tried to steady her voice.

"It's me, Mark. Aunt Bella and Uncle Frank are leaving in less than an hour. I was hoping we could have breakfast together."

Mark, she breathed. Sweet, gentle and attentive Mark. He was so much more along the lines of what she wanted—so much more maneuverable—a little voice goaded her.

She went down to breakfast escorted by Mark and tried not to limp, the excruciating pain just bearable.

"Here she is," Mark announced to Bella and Frank who were finishing up their coffee and toast. "I told you I'd bring her down."

"Sarah!" exclaimed Bella. "You look so pale and tired. Are you ill?"

"I didn't sleep well."

"You may be coming down with…something," Frank supplied, giving her an odd glance. "I feel responsible for causing this. I hope you can forgive me."

"Don't be silly, Professor. It has nothing to do with you. I hope you are feeling better." Sarah smiled at him kindly.

Frank Minsk nodded at her, inviting her attention.

Sarah looked at him squarely and felt as naked as when she had first woken up that morning. Why did it seem as if he knew? Could that fool Julian have said something?

"Jeff is on his way," added Bella. "You should eat a little. It will make you feel better."

Mark handed her coffee, a muffin and a small bowl of fruit.

Sarah smiled at him in gratitude. He was terribly kind and handsome, and this went a long way to restoring her faith in human nature.

"Julian took the children to town," Bella told her with a smile. "There is a little fair at the park this morning, with ponies and clowns—it will do Melissa good to be less precocious and more childlike."

At once, Bella's words descended on her like a gentle breeze dissipating an impending giant storm cloud. Julian was away, out of the house. The sun was bright and warm again. "Melissa is a gifted child, isn't she?"

"That she is," Frank murmured.

Bella smiled and nodded.

On the way back Frank was silent, Sara noticed, which wasn't like his usual behavior. She hoped it was due to his heart palpitations of the previous evening and not, as she worried, that he suspected about her and Julian.

CHAPTER THREE

A few days later Sarah met with her cousin Nicky in Central Park, at the Bethesda Fountain. Summer was approaching in all areas of the park and New York overflowed with the scent of new buds and wild flowers. The park's denizens walked, jogged, skated and rode their bikes with renewed ardor. Better yet, the rebirth served to waylay Sarah's thoughts of one tortuous Saturday evening, barely four days past. She desperately needed to clear her head to better prepare for the upcoming concert a mere two weeks away.

They sat down on one of the benches, both peeling the wrapper off giant pretzels they had purchased from the nearby vendor.

Nicky was one of five cousins—her favorite one—the only daughter of her Uncle John and Aunt Karen. John Miller was one of her father's brothers. Sarah had stayed with them during the scholastic season, when first coming to New York to study at Julliard four years earlier.

"So, any news from him?" Nicky asked about Julian.

"No. You don't know how much I wish I could go back and undo that pathetic evening, Nicky."

"Why? Seems to me you experienced the best sex of your life. Not many of us ever get to live through moments like that. Cherish them."

"Don't be silly. A normal person makes love when they're in love, not as though it's consumed in vengeance, to prove a point. Performed under those conditions, of course sparks are going to fly. In the end, though, it ends up meaning very little."

"That sounds right out of a book. What's your basis for comparison? One, maybe two weak and tepid love affairs?"

Sarah hesitated. She looked at Nicky and shook her head with a shrug of her shoulders.

Nicky laughed. "That's precious. Don't tell me you're a—were—a virgin, because I won't believe you. You're twenty-four years old for shit's sake. You had to have a high school sweetheart—the prom—always a biggie," Nicky continued, staring at her with wide-eye amazement.

"I never had a prom. I had tutors, remember? Old ugly ones."

"Yeah, right. Sorry, I forgot," Nicky answered sheepishly. "But you were engaged to a Frenchmen of all people.

They never take no for an answer."

"Not Serge; he took no for an answer very well. He was patient enough for the sex part. It's the getting married he wanted us to do as soon as possible."

"Did I ever tell you how abnormal that is? All guys ever want to do is have sex. It's a biological function. Meanwhile, no guy is ever in a hurry to get married, unless he's planning to use marriage as a cover. He's gay, doesn't want anybody to know, marries the girl next door. He's foreign, doesn't want anybody to know, marries a patriotic girl. He's poor, doesn't want anybody to know, marries a girl with money…Oh, my God!" Nicky put her hand over her mouth.

"Don't even suggest it. If Serge had been interested in my inheritance, he would have waited until I was twenty-five. I don't get a penny 'til then, except for the meager allowance my trust fund provides me once a month."

Nicky took a long look at Sarah. "You really were a virgin?"

"Yes. *Was* is the operative word. The sad part is that I could have fallen in love with Mark, Julian's brother. It could still happen. We're going out on Friday. But now, I can't ever be with him."

"Why not?"

"Can you see me telling him that his brother ravished me—that he was the first man in my life? The very first man I made love with? I am apt to start a family feud that would last for generations to come."

"Why does he have to know?"

"People in love don't have secrets."

"Something else you've read in a book. Anyway, this Julian didn't ravish you. You told me, in tears, the very next day that you were the one who'd insisted he go through with it."

"That's why I am so humiliated. I can't believe I did that."

"You weren't drugged or anything…were you?"

"No. I can't even use the excuse that I was drunk. Maybe he just bullied me into it. I don't know. He was so insatiable. The fact that he was big and powerful…I just turned to mush." Sarah shivered in the hot mid-day sun.

"Ooh! He sounds yummy in the tummy. Hey! There's a peddler with drinks; do you want one? All this talk is making me thirsty." Nicky was a brown-haired, blue-eyed cutie with freckles on the bridge of her nose. Where men were concerned, she was incorrigible. "Don't move. You just sit, I'll get the drinks."

"I'll have lemonade. Thanks, Nicky," Sarah answered.

Nicky bought them from a pimple-faced adolescent wielding a bike and a freezer.

"There you go." Nicky handed her the drink and straw. "Does it still…hurt?"

Sarah shook her head, dangerously close to tears.

"Listen," Nicky tried to soothe her. "It's not all that bad. I mean, did you ever stop to think that hate is just next door to love and that maybe you secretly have feelings for this guy. That would make it okay—wouldn't it?"

"If you mean it would make me less of a lush—then yes. It would be preferable if I had feelings for him. Only, I don't..."

"Wait a minute. I think you just might." Nicky gave her a sidelong glance.

Sarah threw her a disgusted leer. She could not tell if Nicky was using her predicament to make fun, or if she was reveling in another of her wacky ideas.

"Hear me out. Don't give me the evil eye just yet," Nicky told her good humouredly. "Let me paint you a better picture—a complete one. Now, you have a fiancée for two years, in the most romantic city in the world—Paris, France. This...Serge doesn't try to get to home base with you and..."

"No, no. He tried—on several occasions. He was just never disrespectful of my feelings."

"It's not Serge's behavior I'm talking about here—although any Frenchman who is respectful of a woman's feelings to the point of turning down sex is a discredit to his countrymen, let me tell you. There are many ways to entice a woman to have sex and still respect her feelings. But that's another story. What I'm saying is that if you never had these inexplicable, humiliating and all consuming urges with your fiancée, if you were able to resist the brother, Mark,...isn't it just possible that this man is a force of nature because he is your destiny?"

"Now you're the one that sounds like a book," Sarah smiled, "a psychology book. Am I your next assignment?"

"Well, you are good subject matter, that's for sure. Only, since I'm in my third year, you wouldn't be good practice." Nicky threw her a glance that drew Sarah's attention. "Your situation is classic text book material of the first year variety."

"I disagree," Sarah told her with a smile. "I think Freud would support me in this. It was never my childhood fantasy to fall in love with a rough, egomaniacal oaf who would rather have sex than make love."

"You don't know this for sure. Okay, he made incendiary moves on you..." Nicky fanned herself with her half eaten pretzel, feigning loss of consciousness. "But he did have his tender moments," she smiled, "you told me. You said that the two of you spoke softly, like lovers, at 3:00 in the morning—or did you just dream that part?"

"We did talk. He seemed interested at the time. Looking back, though, I think he was more shy than interested. He asked about my life; I told him I'd been orphaned, that my parents had died when I was four. I explained about the inheritance my mother was due to receive from her father, but then didn't—you know, the crash—my grandfather's broken heart. He's the one who remarked that my mother was my age, actually, when she died in that train wreck."

"See! Now that's an interested man."

"But when I tried to give him advice about Melissa and

Brad and the disadvantages of studying at home, he clammed up. He ignored me completely. Instead, he bent and tongue-kissed my navel, opening the floodgates to more sex and lust. I don't really know when we stopped. All I know is that I woke up in the guest bedroom, without any clothes. And he was nowhere. At the time, I was ecstatic not to have to face him. That would have been so humiliating. But now, I'm thinking that he ran and hid like the king-rat that he is."

"Vin Diesel! I don't know. When you say he looks like Vin Diesel, it's hard for me to sympathize with you, cous'. I think you should have treated him better."

"How? He was out the door and out of my life before I had anything to say about it—and now that I do have something to say about it, I say good riddance."

"Maybe he knew you'd be embarrassed and wanted to spare you in front of the others. Hey! Do you think that maybe he realized you were a virgin and was so ashamed, he's gone off to some distant part of the world to expiate his sins?"

"No. But the thought of him distant and expiating is a comforting one. I don't want to talk about him anymore. He's out of my life; and all I am going to do from now on is practice for my up-coming concert. Starting Monday, I have to rejoin the orchestra, which will mean putting in full days. I will have a lot less free time on my hands. Good riddance to Julian Spinner."

"What about the brother, Mark Spinner?"

Sarah sighed, smiling as she imagined Mark's handsome face.

"This is me, the psychology major again…Did you ever wonder why Mark—who is supposedly interested in you—has never asked about you? Who you are, what you're about…what you like?"

Nicky was going to be a good psychologist, Sarah surmised. Those were indeed very good questions.

Before she had time to answer, Sarah's cell phone rang. "Sarah Miller?"

"Miss Miller, this is Lieutenant Crenshaw. We've made some progress on your case and we'd like you to come down and give us a hand this afternoon. Is that possible?"

"More line-up identifications?" Sarah glanced at Nicky.

"It's okay. I'll go with you," Nicky whispered.

"I'll be there, Lieutenant, in an hour or so."

Precisely one hour later, Sarah and Nicky climbed the steps of the 19th Precinct, on 67th Avenue and proceeded to locate Lieutenant Crenshaw's office. Sarah knew the drill. This was her third time there in the last four months. The police were vigilantly trying to find the hit-and-run driver she had seen so clearly, just seconds before he had struck her down. She had suffered a bruised ankle and hip, and torn ligaments in her left wrist. She had been extremely lucky.

The police station was like an active hive, uniforms and laymen darting left and right. Clashing with their dingy surroundings, the tall ethereal musician that was Sarah and the cute bouncy personality that was Nicky got a few traditional wolf whistles from some of the locals. Even the officer at the desk was grateful when he saw them heading his way.

Sarah identified herself at the desk, for form since young Henry Jigs was always charmed to see her. But swamped with work, the star-struck officer in charge assigned a young policewoman to escort them to Arthur Crenshaw's office.

Up a few stairs, Arthur Crenshaw's office was more like a tiny cubicle with four walls that didn't quite reach the ceiling.

"Have a seat, ladies," he told them in a strong New York drawl. Turning toward the young officer who had guided their way there, he added, "Norma, get another chair for…the friend, Miss…"

"…Nicky Miller. I'm Sarah's cousin."

Once Norma had brought them another chair, had left and closed the door behind her, Crenshaw stared at Sarah, waiting for her to speak her mind.

"I came today, Lieutenant," Sarah told him at once, "but starting Monday, I will be rejoining the orchestra. It will be difficult for me to take time off and help you with your investigation."

"I understand. We'd like you to check a few more people. Once you've done that, we'll talk."

Sarah thought that sounded strange. Nevertheless, they got up when Crenshaw did, and she, Nicky and the lieutenant rejoined Norma waiting outside the office to accompany them to the screening room. Tucked away behind the one-way mirror, she examined the seven people they had rounded up. This time, Sarah recognized the young blond man she had glimpsed before the impact, his beady eyes and unshaven face forever imbedded in her mind.

"You're absolutely sure he's your hitter?" Crenshaw asked her, both his hands leaning on the table in front of him.

"I'll never forget that face, Lieutenant—or his eyes. I'm sure," Sarah told him, visibly shaken by the find.

"Because now I gotta to tell you, the case is going to Detective Cox. He's homicide. He's the one going to do the leg work on this one from now on."

Sarah and Nicky looked at each other. "Why? Homicide…what does that mean exactly?"

"Detective Cox will tell you himself. He's waiting for you. His office is on the second floor. Norma will take you." Crenshaw rounded the corner of the small anti-chamber to the witness room, stuck his head out the door and bellowed to be heard over the noise in the basement area of the precinct. "Norma!" Without checking for results, he extended a hand, first to Sarah, then to Nicky. "I hope everything works out for you, Miss Miller."

This conversation did not bode well, but Sarah decided to remain positive. There was no point in panicking before she heard all the facts.

Norma led them upstairs—second floor, this time. As they approached Detective Cox's office, Sarah saw a familiar face through the glass wall. She froze, nervously clutching Nicky's arm. She tried to speak as Nicky asked her what was wrong, but nothing came out of her mouth. She was riveted to the spot. From somewhere, she heard Norma bid them to sit and wait for Detective Cox who would be with them shortly. All she could do was stand and stare at the man in Cox's office.

"Sarah, will you please tell me what's wrong?" Nicky was becoming impatient.

"It's him. The man facing Detective Cox is Julian Spinner." Sarah's voice was a one-breath whisper, and as she continued to stare at his profile, her heart banged repeated somersaults inside her chest until she felt nauseous and weak.

Nicky helped her sit down. Then she stared at the man her cousin loathed, the man who had claimed her with such willful determination that he could still make her shake, four days later.

Julian stood, walked across to shake the detective's hand, and suddenly faced the girls as he turned to leave.

"My God! Is he ever gorgeous, Sarah. I can't believe you did it with him—all night!" Nicky was mesmerized. "He's a hunk and a half!" she breathed.

Sarah poked her in the ribs. She couldn't believe that Nicky was mentioning this now.

Julian stopped in front of them. When he glanced at

Sarah, he immediately lost his smile. He stared into her eyes, a wayward muscle flexing in his jaw. "How are you, Sarah?" His voice was low and soft.

It took all of Sarah's strength to stare back at him, smile and remain casual. "I've been well—all things considered…"

These last words seemed to spike some life into him. He gave her a mocking crooked smile. "I'm glad to hear you've been considering…things. An ounce of prevention…they say."

Sarah's wits were too scattered for her to think, to add anything coherent, her focus directed on retaining as normal a pose as she could.

"If you'll excuse us," Nicky told him, starry-eyed and all smiles, "the detective is waiting for us." She pulled Sarah away with her. As she did, she noticed Julian remained in the hallway, watching Sarah walk into Cox's office—as if he could maintain eye contact by staring intently at the back of her.

Cox answered the phone as they walked in. This gave Sarah a pause to regroup.

"Is he gone?" she whispered to Nicky.

Nicky checked, then nodded that he was. She heard Sarah's deep intake of breath and smiled to herself. Now that she was much more aware of the situation, she would have a few things to discuss with Sarah.

"Thank you for coming in, Miss Miller. I'm Detective Ray Cox. Would you like some coffee?"

Sarah shook her head, still frazzled from coming face

to face with Julian. "Lieutenant Crenshaw said something about…homicide? He said you would explain."

Cox sat back in his chair, swiveling from side to side while fidgeting with the pen on his desk. "When will you be twenty-five, Miss Miller?" he asked unexpectedly.

"In six months. Why do you ask?"

"We've had a young couple, newlyweds, come forward with information on your hitter. They didn't want to get involved—managed to stay low and ease their conscience for the past four months. Now the wife is pregnant, they want to do the right thing. They tell us they were there; they saw the whole thing."

"And…"

"They claim it wasn't an accident."

"I…I don't understand…what does that mean exactly? That someone deliberately tried to run me down?" Sarah snickered. "I don't think I'm that famous—or even that popular." She glanced at Nicky, who had a stricken look in her eyes but who reached out to hold her hand. "Detective, these people made a mistake. Why would anyone want to…? Are you saying someone wants to kill me?" Sarah sat further back in her chair, the wind suddenly knocked out of her. That there could be someone out there, planning her death.

"What you're telling me, Miss Miller, is that you think this isn't possible?"

"Yes. That's exactly what I'm telling you, Detective. It's impossible."

"You don't know of anyone who would have any interest in harming you or taking you out of the picture, for any reason?"

"Absolutely none. I lead a very simple life. I enjoy the company of a few friends; I bury myself in my work...Detective Cox, I'm twenty-four years old. I haven't had time to make any worthwhile enemies."

"Wait a minute, Detective..."

"Who are you?"

"I'm Nicky Miller, Sarah's cousin. Why did you want to know about her twenty-fifth birthday? Does this have anything to do with her inheritance?"

"Bull's eye! Miss Nicky, bull's eye! Now, we're not sure, mind you. Spinner's the one who brought it up. When he did, he didn't know about the couple coming forward with their information—none of us did. Now that we do, his theory makes more sense. But don't worry. We're on the case."

Sarah could not believe she had heard right. "Spinner! Julian Spinner?"

"Uh huh. You know him?"

Sarah's face paled. She tried not to purse her lips and sound livid. 'What does he have to do with me or my case?"

"He knows of you. He's a big fan of yours," Cox smiled. "He came to us months ago with this theory, the very next week after reading about the hit in the papers. We should have paid more attention."

Months ago! He's a big fan! He knew me when I went

there that day. He tricked me. Sarah could not reason anything else.

"I don't understand," Nicky interrupted, glancing worriedly at Sarah. "Is he a police officer?"

"Nah. Him and I grew up together. We went to the same school. He hung around one crowd, going one way; I hung around another, going my way. Ten years later—five years ago—he's a successful businessman looking to put back into the community…know what I mean? Turns out he has his ear to the ground. He knows how to collect information. Thugs know him. They respect him. We use it here at the station. He's helped close some of our cold case files, and he takes some of them punk repeaters we're ready to throw away; teaches them karate—makes something out of them—some of them, anyway. Knows how their minds click." The detective wiggled a hand to his temple to better illustrate.

Sarah was speechless. Julian had appeared interested in her—that night—that stupid, foolish night; here she had thought he was just making small talk, filling the empty spaces.

"This morning, the newlys identified the same guy you just picked out of the line-up. They saw him get in the car, wait for you to show up and then ram you down." Cox spoke with his hands on a subject that was still too raw for Sarah's nerves. His ramblings were stated so matter-of-factly and in such a New York monotone drawl that she felt as though she was eavesdropping on someone else's predicament.

"So what now?" Nicky asked, just recovering her senses.

"We've got six months to find whoever is behind this. I mean, we'll convict this kid—keep him in; but what good will that do? They'll just send somebody else."

"What do you propose my cousin do? She can't go back to her apartment, obviously. She can't just pick up her life and pretend nothing's wrong."

"No, Ma'am, she can't."

Sarah got up and began pacing, wringing her hands as if to extract some form of plan from the long, slender fingers.

"You can stay with us, Sarah. We're on the West Side, close to Lincoln Center," she added for Cox' benefit. "You can share my room, like we used to a couple of years ago, remember?"

"Of course I remember, sweetie. I'm not dumb, just… dumbfounded—whatever that means." Sarah knew Nicky was trying to make her feel better, to give her courage. She loved her for it. "But that won't work, Nicky."

"Why not?"

"Detective, you seem to think that this is because of my inheritance?"

"Fat chance, it is."

"Then, this would mean it would have to be someone or something that gets the money if I…I die, true?"

"That's the general consensus."

"These people will have done their homework. They will know of Nicky and my uncle's house…"

"If you know who's responsible, why not arrest them now?" Nicky asked.

"First of all, we only have an idea—a vague one at that. Then we have to be able to make it stick in court. We need proof. The good news is that they don't know we're onto them. They still think we are treating this like a hit-and-run. The bad news is that we might have to work with Interpol on this—which means slower results."

"Interpol?" Nicky was surprised.

"If our perpetrator is in Europe, then it becomes an international problem."

"Isn't upgrading the case to a homicide red-flagging it a bit?" Nicky wanted to know.

"Only you and Crenshaw know about this, and of course the department. Listen, Miss Miller, if it is any consolation, we have a man assigned to you 24/7. He's plain clothes, and has been with you diligently for the past three days…"

"Your department can afford to put a detective on me twenty-four hours a day?" Sarah was amazed with their resources. The city's finest were forever complaining that they didn't have any money.

"We delve into anonymous donations from time to time. It will be fine for a while. That's not what you should be worrying about, Miss Miller. We suggest that you stay away from your apartment. Go to a friend—a relative's home—if at all possible."

"That's easier said than done, Detective. I don't have many friends. I have my family and that's all."

"I beg to differ," he added, trying to be chipper. "The Spinners have offered to have you stay with them. They have a huge house in Long Island and Julian's going to be working with us on this one anyway," he shrugged.

Sarah put her hand in front of her mouth to stifle a startled scream. Turning away from Cox, she began to laugh nervously, silently at first, her shoulders rising and falling so that it looked as though she was crying.

Nicky put an arm around her shoulders and realized Sarah was adrift with giddy bursts of laughter, emitting slight hiccups whenever she came up for air. "Oh! Nicky, that's rich…" she managed to utter between two gulps of air.

Nicky squeezed her hard, trying to distract her from speaking in front of this policeman.

"Can we go now, Detective? Sarah is very tired and needs to examine her feelings with all of this, you understand."

Cox got up and nodded. "If you need anything or have any questions, I am here. Here's my card with my direct line and my home phone number. Nothing's too good for a friend of Julian's."

This was the last straw. Nicky thanked the detective, scooped Sarah out of there into the hall and out the front door as fast as she could.

By now, Sarah was laughing hysterically. Coming up for air every now and then, she was holding her sides; they were fast becoming tender and painful. "The man…the man…" she swallowed a few hiccups, but couldn't stop laughing long enough to make a proper sentence. She fanned her face, hoping to delay the next burst.

Nicky felt like slapping her. Instead, she shook the hell out of her and waited for the last dregs of laughter to subside. "Please pull yourself together, Sarah. We need to think this through, sweetie."

"I'm sorry. It was just so funny, the irony." She wiped her eyes with a tissue. "It's rich. Too rich for my blood, they would say in the movies. Did you hear what he said? The man who ravished me is kind enough to put me up, he says—so that I don't get hurt. Any friend of Julian…Oh! Nicky! Why is my life so upside down? What did I do to deserve this?"

"Come on. We're going to Serendipity. I'm treating you to ice cream."

That didn't seem strong enough to calm her nerves, Sarah thought. But if nothing else, it would cool her off. She began laughing again, thinking about applying ice cream to raw nerves to cool them down.

CHAPTER FOUR

By the time the waitress had assigned them a table, Sarah had calmed down and was searching through bits of memory to help her make sense of it all.

"Hey," Nicky smiled. "Maybe I should enter the Marylyn Monroe look-alike contest. What do you think—do you think I'd win?" Nicky indicated the billboard write-up on the wall with a toss of her head. It got a smile out of Sarah.

It was good. Sarah needed a place to land. Light was good.

"Hi, my name is Jane. What will you ladies have?" Jane flashed a bright smile.

Sarah smiled and ordered first. "I'll have the Raro Pecan Pie and a cinnamon coffee, thank you."

"The Frrrozen Pineapple Lime for me, thanks. You're not having the YuDuFunDu Fruit and Fudge?" Nicky asked, once their waitress had left.

Sarah wrinkled her nose and shook her head. "It wouldn't sit right just now." She refused to spoil her favorite dessert on such a sad occasion.

"Can we talk about this now?" Nicky wanted to know.

Sarah nodded hesitantly.

"No. I mean really dig, without the gloves…"

"Yes, of course. You're being silly."

"…dig down and dirty, with picks and shovels." Nicky's blue eyes rounded like quarters.

Sarah eyed her with playful green ones. "Yes, you can scold me all you want. I won't be angry. Is that what you wanted to hear?"

Nicky smiled. "You start," she told Sarah.

"I just can't believe the man knew me. He's a fan—that detective said. He tricked me into making love to him…"

"Is that the urgency that's on your mind right now? You've just been told that someone out there wants to kill you, and all you can do is find new ways to sleaze Julian Spinner?"

"I'm pathetic, I know. I just can't shake the feeling I was used."

"First off, don't ever say again that the man ravished you. Not after what I saw today, outside that office."

"Not true. Didn't you see how he laughed at me—*considering things—ounce of prevention*?"

"He wasn't laughing at you, sweetie—laughing yellow

maybe. What I saw was a man exceedingly nervous, painfully ashamed and hopelessly in love."

"You're a rosy-eyed romantic, Nicky. You always were. He went to the police about my case even before I met him."

"...Which proves that he had your best interests at heart, well before you two...did it. What was his motive then, huh? Anyway, your case—that's what you should be focusing on right now."

"You're right. But now Julian is a part of that too, isn't he?"

"First sense you've made all afternoon."

"Why would you say he's in love with me?"

"It's so obvious, Sarah. That look he gave the back of you when I dragged you into the office...the hurt, the hunger in his eyes...it was so...just so deep. My heart ached for him—for his misery."

"Well, I'm the one who needs your sympathy now." A bite of her delicious pie brought Sarah little comfort.

"Come live with us," Nicky urged. "It'll just be for a while. We can go to the conservatory together, like old times. Whoever the guardian angel is that's tailing you, he'll continue to do so wherever you live."

It sounded like the proper thing to do. Sarah took a sip of her coffee. "I've been living where I am for the past year now; eight months before the accident, four months since the accident. Why would anyone attempt anything now, when they had all the time to do so before today?"

"I think what the detective omitted saying is now that they've arrested the kid who ran you down, the people who hired him might feel the urgency of...trying again using someone else—someone no one will see coming." Nicky's pretty eyes squinted as if feeling the fear her words might cause.

"You're right, Nicky. I hadn't thought of that. Ray Cox should've warned me." *Or does he even realize it himself?* "Okay, this is what I'll do. I'll go home and get a few things to sleep at your place tonight—then we'll see how it pans out for the next week or so," Sarah added.

"Great! I'll help you."

Sarah shook her head. "No. Don't waste your time. I have errands to run and things to do at home first. "I'll take a cab to your place later. I promise," Sarah insisted when she saw Nicky's doubting Thomas face.

Sarah and Nicky parted ways near 76th Street. Nicky was headed West Side and Sarah hopped a bus north.

Walking to her building, Sarah looked behind her, checking both sides of the street to try to catch a glimpse of the plain clothes policeman who was supposed to protect her. He knew how to remain invisible; she saw no one.

In her building's lobby, Mrs. Kolinsky was chatting with Jorge, the tall clerk at the front desk who acted as security. Sarah wondered if the police department had approached Jorge as a precautionary measure, handing out clues on how to best protect her and her apartment. Maybe the officer had identified himself to Jorge. Someone lurking around the building was apt to call attention to himself. It was best to warn any concerned party. But Jorge smiled, gawking at her openly as usual without so much as a frown or a line on his forehead.

She walked down her hallway, cursing the thirty-watt light bulbs. Conserving energy was commendable. Preserving her eyesight she deemed more important. But complain as she may, the landlord's only solution had simply been to offer her the use of a small flashlight.

She rummaged for her keys and applied them to three separate locks. She had learned her first month in New York that it paid to discourage the amateur thief with an annoying number of locks. The trouble was it annoyed her even more.

She turned on the light in the foyer, dropped her purse and keys on the little hall table, glancing as she did at her reflection in the mirror, and let out a scream. She saw the vague dark outline of an intruder in the mirror and twisted to face him, fear paralyzing her to the spot. It was worse than she imagined. She recognized the perpetrator.

"What are you doing here? How did you get in? Who let you in—NO! Don't you dare come near me or I'll scream..."

"Relax. I won't touch you. I won't hurt you. Just hear me out, please."

Julian's eyes were darker than she had ever seen them. His face was a pack of nerves and she remembered what Nicky had told her—about his misery, so deep, she had said it was. She forgot about her fear when she noticed the pain on his face, and she nodded, affirming that she would listen but urging him with her hand to stay back.

"Can you please sit, Sarah—at the other end of the room, if you must?"

The end of the room was much too close. But it was more of a request than a demand, so Sarah complied, sitting on the edge of the chair, prim and proper, but refusing to look directly at him.

"First," she spoke in a small voice she had difficulty recognizing, "how did you get into my apartment?"

He gave her a pale smile. "I wasn't always a successful businessman. I had a rough childhood, learned a few tricks."

So much for Jorge's security—or that policeman's for that matter. Where was he, she wondered.

She finally peaked at the whole of him as he got up and began pacing. She closed her eyes and felt a strange stirring in the pit of her stomach. Nicky had called him a hunk. It wasn't that he was good looking—not like Mark. Julian was more virile, extremely magnetic—probably used to drawing female attention, she thought ruefully.

He was pacing, but silent, as though he could not find the words. "I want to apologize for…last Saturday. I was wrong and I take all the blame for what happened between us."

Sarah winced when she noticed how humble he was. This was a Julian she had not had the pleasure of meeting.

"I haven't slept in four days, Sarah. Partly because I keep reliving what happened between us—I've never had that kind of...well, whatever that was. You have to admit it was strong. Now I am paying for it because it's with me all the time," he breathed heavily.

His apology was more like a poke in the wounds and it angered her more than the lack of one.

"You call this an apology? You just want me to feel sorry for you and your poor unsatiated lust."

"No. No. That's not what I want. I'm doing this wrong..." He dropped his head in his hands.

"Anyway, I don't know why you're being all magnanimous. I'm the one who...who...who wouldn't say no." Sarah bit her lip but the tears still came. She jabbed at them quickly with her fists and stared at him, head high, as rebellious as ever.

Julian was attempting to restore Sarah's dignity by exposing as much as he could of his own raw emotions—making himself the vulnerable target—when what he truly wanted to do was sweep her up in his arms and kiss the hurt out of her if it took ten, twenty, one hundred nights like the first one they had had together.

He sat back down, mostly to be at eye level with her. For a long time, his eyes caressed her own teary ones until he felt she was relaxed and prepared to listen. "Just the fact that I am here, Sarah—and please don't interrupt me until I've finished—please?"

She nodded, hypnotized by the look in his dark eyes.

"Just the fact that I'm sitting here with you, that I have to hold back from touching you...I'm not a man of words, Sarah. I'm more the guy who does..."

"...And takes..."

He smiled. "And takes," he added good-humouredly. "Sarah," he continued, barely louder than a whisper, "I've been a fan of yours since I first heard you perform, two years ago, at Julliard. There was a whole band—a whole orchestra. I only saw you, only heard you."

Her demeanor softened considerably. She found herself staring at his mouth and she took a ragged breath. The heat she had experienced the other night was back, lodged in her lower limbs and traveling upward in a big hurry.

"Sarah, I fell in love with you the first minute I saw you. Hopelessly, irrevocably, for better or for worse...in love."

"You have a funny way of showing it," she said softly, more to fill in the awkward pause that followed. So Nicky had read him correctly.

"When Mark told me you were coming, it didn't click. I never listen to him in person—much less over the phone. But when I saw you standing there, I panicked. At first, I thought my Aunt Bella had learned of my feelings for you and that she and you had concocted some cruel, humiliating matchmaking game—laughing at my expense—pitying this poor bastard of a man who hasn't had a relationship in the last three years..." He sighed, hiding his eyes with his hands.

Sarah swallowed an awful lump in her throat. She was suddenly achingly aware of the mortification this big man was putting himself through for her. If she extended her arm and a hand, she would be able to stroke the soft, shiny crown of his head. She stiffened her back and sat up straighter. This is how she had gotten in this mess to begin with.

He resurfaced, his eyes extremely brilliant. "The real heartache came when I realized that there was no...game, no specific...wanting to be with me. You preferred Mark. That's when I realized that the first sting had been much easier to bear. Mark is notorious with getting his way with beautiful women. I knew I'd never stand a chance. Then I reasoned myself into thinking that I didn't care; that you were easy—a tease; that you deserved what was coming to you because of the way you were treating me...taunting me...I know, I know," he forestalled her. "You were reacting to my behavior. Anyway, I didn't start off to do what I did...in my room—that was pretty desperate of me."

Sarah crossed over to sit beside him. She placed a hand on his while staring deep into his eyes. "It was just as much my fault. Only I didn't understand—I couldn't understand—that I was baiting you, teasing, as you mentioned. I assure you, Julian, I am not a tease..."

"Please go back to sit where you were," he told her gruffly, the tenderness gone from his demeanor.

She did as he asked, losing her smile in the process.

"I know you're not a tease, Sarah. You weren't even

very knowledgeable. Don't get me wrong," he added quickly, noticing the hurt look on her face. "You're an exceedingly quick study," he added, emphasizing his words with a hungry moan. "But the next morning, when I brought you back to the guest room…that's when I realized that…well, you know."

"That I was a virgin?" Sarah asked him, her head high and her chin up. "How?"

"The sheet…"

"I see," she added, her cheeks changing color. "Why admit all this, Julian? What is it that you want from me?" Did he want her to tell him that she loved him too? She was not going to lie. Not to save his dignity, not even to save his heart. She considered the truth the best remedy she could afford him.

"I want a truce between us," he smiled, his eyes caressing her red cheeks. "I want you to come to stay at our house in Long Island. I'll pay for whatever cost you incur to attend recitals or practices or just to come into the city—at least, until we can clear up your problem. Ray is very close to doing so. Trust me."

"I don't know, Julian. There's Mark."

Sarah got up and began walking toward the open kitchen. An eating counter separated the two areas and Julian took a seat on one of the stools, watching as she prepared a kettle for tea.

"He is very…enterprising—to use a kind word," she smiled. "Don't think that I'm complaining; he is charming.

It's just that after what's happened between you and I, how could I ever tell him…?"

"Why would you have to? He'll never hear it from me, I can guarantee that."

"Two people in love aren't supposed to have secrets…" She stopped, just realizing what she had admitted. The look on Julian's face tore the heart out of her chest.

"Are you in love with Mark, Sarah?"

She shook her head, vigorously. "No. I hardly know him…" She did not finish. There was no point.

"But it could happen, is that what you're saying?"

She shrugged and put a few tea bags in the pot. All she knew was that she did not wish to hurt this man. If something was to develop between Mark and her, then they did not have to parade it brazenly. There would be time enough to settle with the fiddler later, she decided. For now, she would be discreet.

"I want you to be safe, Sarah. I'm here to help you pack and take you back with me."

She could not imagine this wall of a man elbow-deep in her personal things. She had a difficult enough time visualizing the forty-five minute ride with him to Long Island. He made her feel edgy and uncomfortable. The memory of his tongue traveling over her body was still readily pulsating through her senses. When he was near her like this, the image of him taking her passionately, wantonly with persistent stubborn strength was digitalized in her brain. And suddenly, the words he had spoken during the heated strokes echoed back to her with crystalline clarity. She remembered now. He had told her he loved her, repeatedly, feverishly, throughout the course of the night.

"Yes, you may help me pack. And yes, I will return with you, Julian."

She turned away from him, glad the counter was there to support her, and closed her eyes waiting for the dizziness to dissipate. She could not understand where this overwhelming need to say yes to him came from.

Shrinking against the passenger door in Julian's Grand Cherokee Jeep, Sarah tried desperately to avoid contact with the man's big shoulder and couldn't believe how much room he took. She stared out the window, but the sun had gone down an hour earlier, and all she could see in some well-lit spots was her frightened reflection staring back at her.

It might have taken her forever to pack. But even though having Julian's hands in the midst of her personal belongings was disheartening, he had been helpful, especially fast and focused—where she might have fiddled and dawdled. She did not particularly wish to leave, evidenced by her snail's tempo that had driven Julian to the brink of impatience.

Nicky had been duly shocked to see them arrive on her doorstep. Sarah had thought it better to tell her in person exactly where she was going. And though she had been supportive of Sarah and her anxieties—when they had conversed privately—she had still gone out of her way to be pleasant and all smiles to Julian. As for Julian, he had been taciturn but polite.

"I'm sorry if I wasn't more pleasant to your cousin, Sarah. I have a lot on my mind; and small talk was never my strong suit."

This she could believe. She imagined that his lack of communication might have been the catalyst for his failed marriage. She certainly would find it difficult to live with the fact that the love of her life could not express himself clearly.

"Sarah? Are you all right?" He glanced at her, thinking she might be sleeping.

They were in such close quarters that it not only made her jittery, it kept her unsettled and strangely irritated.

"I'm fine," she answered in a small voice.

"Do you need me to stop?" His voice was solicitous and urgent, which just annoyed her more.

"I told you. I'm fine." She sighed deeply, chancing a glance in his direction. "I'm just uncomfortable about all this." *I don't think there can ever be small talk between us.* She saw his jaw contract and turned quickly, before her senses could betray her. "It's...too soon," she relented, her voice a tad softer.

"I know that you're scared," he added, misreading her last statement. "But don't be. I won't let anything happen to you, Sarah, I promise. In a few days, we'll know more. Cox is working with Interpol and he's requested a copy of your grandfather's will."

"You think the will might shed some light on who's to blame?"

"It might," he answered gently.

"Does Mark know—why I'm coming to stay?"

"I briefed him last night. He wanted to pick you up. I declined. There was no point in both of us being there—I hope you don't mind?" he asked as an afterthought.

She didn't mind. She shook her head. "What do you mean, both there…?" Then a thought struck her. "Julian, who is the man they have watching me 24/7, as the detective said?

Julian smiled. "You're looking at him, or at least, at the man in charge of your surveillance."

She shook her head. Was everyone conspiring against her? "Julian, you can't possibly follow me around 24 hours a day. How can you volunteer for a job you know you're not going to be able to do?" So much for protection around the clock, she thought.

He smiled. "I am a businessman who's aching for something to do. I not only have the time, I have the resources; I possess a thorough knowledge of weaponry; and I am a 7th Dan TKD expert and practitioner."

"TKD?" Sarah asked.

"Taekwondo—martial arts."

She sighed. It wasn't his lack of attributes she was worried about; on the contrary. "But Julian, considering what has just happened between us...I mean, to have you in my life, my work, my leisure time...." She closed her eyes, feeling his reaction before she even saw it. She had vowed to think twice before she spoke, especially around him. He had a way of extorting her most private thoughts.

He said nothing but she knew by his sharp intake of breath that he was angry.

The rest of the journey was conducted in cacophonic silence. She was afraid to look at him, and even more frightened to explore her irritated need to lash out at him.

He pulled the jeep into the drive and waited in silence for her to alight. When she did not immediately open her door, he turned in his seat to look at her. Sarah was trying to find the words to express how she felt, but did not want to risk making a bad situation worse.

"Sarah, my volunteering to keep an eye out for you was never meant as a form of...control, or as a way for me to keep tabs on you. My offer to Ray was genuine. I felt I was the best person for the job. Of course, when I did tell Ray I'd do it, I was never going to admit to you how I felt. At your apartment this afternoon, I...you seemed so miserable, so...ashamed, thinking you were responsible...I just blurted out what I thought might make you feel better, and what might make me look less like the ogre you imagine I am. I did it so that we could be friends."

Sarah turned to look at him. He was handsome in his own way, she thought. Imposing strong Julian being consierate and tender was endearing. "What about your feelings?" she asked him softly.

He smiled. "My feelings are my own problem. You're not responsible for the way I feel anymore than you are for the way I plan my life—the way I volunteer my time. What happened last Saturday night is gone, in the past. We can't bring it back anymore than we can erase it. But we can move on and bury it deep—forget about it altogether. That's what I meant by a truce. Can you forgive and forget?"

She took a deep breath, lowering her eyes. She could still remember his mouth applying kisses to the length of her, his body seared to hers. She nodded. "I can forgive, Julian. As for forgetting…" she shrugged. She had to be honest. "It will take some time. I…I still remember…when I close my eyes," she added shyly.

He nodded, promptly opened his door and stepped out. Slamming the door shut, he leaned against the jeep momentarily, allowing the cool metal to lower his temperature gauge, letting the night absorb his pain.

CHAPTER FIVE

Mark was delighted to have Sarah living with them. To enjoy her grace and wit, her poise and beauty across the breakfast table each morning made his day, he never tired of saying.

In the two weeks since she had arrived, little Melissa and she had become good friends. Brad relied on her as well, and the laughter echoed throughout the house frequently. Mark now camped at home most evenings, and when Melissa had asked him where his friend Susan was, Mark had brandished Sarah's hand and proclaimed her his new girlfriend.

Sarah was flattered and touched by their sincere friendship. She was especially pleased with Mark's attentions. But so far they had gone to the movies—with the children, to the scheduled concert at the Alice Tully Hall—with the children, and shopping for summer clothes—with the children. Mark would drive the family station wagon; they would pack the books and the extra sweaters, the water jugs, the camera and the film and head out for their planned destination. It was more adventurous than it was romantic, especially since the only amorous spontaneity Mark and she had shared was a peck on the lips. There had been hugs, tender glances and private conversations, but nothing remotely akin to his first advances of that former Saturday, which to Sarah now seemed eons ago. She liked the snail's paced courtship Mark had adopted. She figured he was making amends for his pushy behavior on that first encounter and was laying the groundwork to building a friendship between them before taking it to the next step.

If he only knew, she sighed. If he knew she had gone on ahead and already taken that step—the whole stair-length in fact—with his brother Julian....Now that she knew him better, she was certain that Mark learning of her predicament would create an enormous rift between the brothers.

As for Julian, she had seen or heard very little of him since the day he had told her he had volunteered to stand guard for her. She left early in the mornings with the transportation he had promised she would have, and came back late in the afternoons. Once she thought she had spotted his jeep driving down Broadway. She had waved but gotten no response. She knew that he had taken charge of her wellbeing, but she did not know if he provided this surveillance himself or if he had entrusted someone else with it. Whoever was watching over her was a perfect shadow. She had not heard or seen the slightest inkling of anyone.

To her surprise, Sarah found she missed Julian's burly presence. Once or twice she had even longed for his wit; for the quick snappy banter they had come to exchange. Mostly, she did not deem it fair that he should extricate himself from his family just to avoid running into her. And once or twice she had glued her ear to his bedroom door for any evidence of his presence, especially on nights when she remembered the torch of sharp dark eyes and the way they had traveled up and down her slender silhouette, bold and unafraid.

Nicky had suggested Sarah hold a frank discussion with him. Why not take him up on his offer of a truce, she had proposed.

But Sarah considered that if Julian stayed away, he needed to distance himself from her, to regroup, recoup, or simply forget about her altogether.

Her constant chewing on this last thought over the last few days brought her shuffling to the communicating bedroom door one night with renewed courage. She glanced at her watch and discovered it was late. But when she listened intently, she heard voices inside. He was on the telephone or listening to television.

She tightened the belt of her robe, ordered her heartbeats to quiet down, took a deep breath, and knocked on his door.

Immediately there was silence.

Julian opened the door with a look of pleasant surprise on his face. He appeared calm and unperturbed. So much for her worrying about him, she rued.

"What can I do for you, Sarah?" he asked with a knowing smile.

Fighting to prevent her cheeks from coloring, she noticed movement behind him. Through the opening Julian was attempting to block, she saw the statuesque profile of a tall woman. She barely had a second to flash on a pretty face. In the space of a breath, the woman had already moved out of view.

"I wanted to know if there were any developments with my case."

"Yes, there have been," he told her, his eyes boring into hers.

He probably knew she had seen the person behind him. But he gave no explanation—no introduction. How dare he bring a girl up to his room—directly next door to hers? She was tempted to stomp off and let the matter drop. But then there would be two of them laughing at her.

"Good, good." Sarah wrung her hands together, trying not to be transparent, wishing she was elsewhere while not wanting this conversation to end. "I placed several calls to Det...Ray Cox. He hasn't returned any of them."

"Ray's been away the last few days. He's coming back on Monday. Tell you what," he added in a kindly manner, "let's have lunch tomorrow and I'll fill you in."

Don't do me any favors, thought Sarah, judging his tone to be condescending. "That's perfect. I have a half day tomorrow. The little deli in front of Carnegie Hall? There's parking there, on Amsterdam."

"No." He gave her a crooked smile. "I'll pick you up, Sarah, in front of the Alice Tully Hall on the corner of Broadway—12:00 sharp. Oh! I'll already have parked."

She nodded.

"Good night, Sarah," he told her, an amused little glint dancing in his eyes, before he closed the door.

It took Sarah a good five minutes to walk away from the door. She was mortified. She had worried about him—his self-admitted loneliness...For someone who had complained about the absence of sexual relationships these last three years, he was sure making up for lost time these past three weeks. First her...then...It was none of her business, she concluded.

Just the same, in bed she instinctively waited to hear Julian's bedroom door open and close. She heard nothing. True, the walls were thick, she thought before stretching out completely, clutching for peace. After tossing and turning, she crouched with bouts of fitful dreams where she was pleading with Julian not to love her, while she waited in the dark for his kisses and soft caresses—calling out his name through a thick metal door.

A noise jerked her awake. She sat up in bed with her heart racing and heard a car revving its motor. She glanced at the night clock beside her bed. She had been asleep for less than an hour. She plopped back down onto the pillows sleepily, ironically thinking Julian had short-changed the tall stranger. An hour in Julian's arms was not enough. Not nearly enough.

The morning found Sarah in a better mood. She had paid particular attention to her appearance. She had applied a red lip-gloss to her full lips and a light dab of coal liner over her eyes. She wore hip-hugging évasé pants paired to a waist-fitted long sleeved blouse that accentuated her shoulders and petite figure. As she walked to the rendezvous area, her long hair swaying to the tempo of her graceful rhythm, many heads twisted and turned following her journey with wistful smiles. One of those heads was Julian's. He saw her pause on the corner of Broadway and search the area thronged with people. His eyes were by far the most wistful as he drank in her beauty and poise, unhurriedly—wondering how he could claim this goddess' heart.

The giant slunk up behind her, making her jump so that when she turned, she tumbled against him.

Quickly she backed away as though burned. "Julian, you scared me. Have you been waiting long?" Sarah stammered.

He laughed at her. "No. I just saw you walk by me. I was leaning against the mailbox." He took her by the hand. His eyes dared her to pull away. She gave him a shy smile as tacit agreement.

Gently he tugged at her as they began walking north on Columbus. "You look shorter," he told her, his eyes scooping her up from head to toe.

"I'm wearing flat sandals. When you said you would be parked, I thought we might have to walk."

"Aren't you the smart one!" He gave her hand a slight squeeze.

"Where are we going?" she asked, trying not to let his toying with her send her reeling.

"It's just four blocks north. The Café des Artistes; it's quiet, subdued, just the place we need to talk privately."

Inside the restaurant, the Maître D welcomed Julian with an open-armed hug. "How's it going, big J? You haven't been here in a while. Not since…"

"Never mind," Julian forestalled him. "Do you have my usual table?"

"When you called me this morning, you didn't give me much time. The Pot au Feu will be ready shortly. Why not take the lovely lady to the Parlor. It doesn't formally open until 5:30, so it'll be quiet there. Carl will serve you drinks until they're ready with your table."

Sarah followed Julian to the Parlor, across the vestibule from the restaurant. She mounted a stool next to him in the quaint mahogany and zinc bar area reminiscent of a Viennese café Serge and she had visited on one of their Eurail jaunts. She had never been in this café before. The old world décor was charming, very French with its murals of females in nude splendor.

She asked Carl for a white wine. He came back with a long stemmed glass for her and a tall glass filled to the brim with a dark pink liquid for Julian.

"People really know you around here. They even know your drink. What is that exactly?"

"This is a favorite concoction of mine," he answered. "Two ounces of cranberry juice, a half jigger of lime and two full measures of Perrier water." He winked at her.

"You look nice today," she attempted. "I've never seen you in a suit before." Sarah wondered where he bought jackets to fit him.

"Thank you. It's not a suit," he answered, undoing the top button, "just a sports jacket."

She nodded, her eyes darting to one side.

"What?" he countered. "Don't look so surprised. I do dress up from time to time."

"I'm not surprised, just…well, not used to it…I guess."

"You're not used to any part of me, Sarah—not yet…" He noticed his words made her uncomfortable. He immediately changed the subject. "I see you are all dolled up too. Lipstick, shiny hair…belly-button showing—very sexy."

"Thank you. It's lip gloss." She smiled. It was her turn to correct him. "We had our pictures taken this morning for one of the seasonal brochures. Sometimes it seems as though there is more promo done than actual music. I guess it's par with the course. One of my professors calls the media and publicity music's commercial expression. He says that without the advertising, music would be silent. It wouldn't fall on the masses' ears—or if it did, no one would know."

"Like the tree—in the forest."

She smiled. "Something like that."

The waiter came to let them know that their table was ready; and Sarah, walking by Julian's side, caught her breath as they entered the old-fashioned homespun beauty of the Christy room. Their table faced the painting entitled The Girl with the Book and displayed a beautiful vase of fresh cut flowers. The waiter had already brought the appetizer, asparagus wrapped with Prosciutto, smoked salmon, and Gravlax. On a side table rested a bottle of red wine and as they sat at their table, another waiter rolled in the pink copper marmite of the Pot au Feu.

"This is extravagant, Julian. To what do I owe the pleasure?" She smiled, her green eyes soft and limpid.

He eyed her intently for a long minute—enough for her to lose the taunting smile. When she lowered her eyes he answered simply, "a guy's got to eat."

She raised her eyebrows, questioning his curt response. Even if his goal was to remain non-committal, he could do better than that.

"All right. I love this place. It's quiet enough for what we have to discuss. The food is excellent…and I only bring here people I find…special. Satisfied?"

Like the lady who was in your room last night? "Satisfied," she nodded.

Julian's smile faded all of a sudden while the onyx in his eyes lost their brilliance. He stared at Sarah intently, put his fork down and took one of her delicate hands in his, studying the long fingers and well-polished nails. "I think, for both our sakes, we should keep our conversation on the subject at hand—the information you asked me for last night."

She did not attempt to remove her hand, but gave him her undivided attention.

"You have to forget about what happened between us that first Saturday we met, Sarah." His voice was curt, but gentle. "You're young, talented, beautiful; you have your whole life ahead of you. You enjoy my brother's company, and I know he more than enjoys yours." He placed her hand gently on the table beside his own. "We are two very different people, Sarah."

"In a way, we are both artists." She thought of his martial arts.

"Are you so hell bent on fighting with me that you're going to argue the case for…" he gestured to the both of them, "us?"

There was so much more she wanted to say. She just didn't want to be misconstrued.

"I thought not," he answered with a complacent smile. His soft icy tone caused her to shiver. She dropped her eyes to her salad. He clearly wanted nothing to do with her—at least not personally. He would help her with the case, protect her, and give her all the information she needed. But he was aiming to forget about that Saturday night. Or had he done so already?

"You have your dreams, your youth...I've already realized most of what I wanted to accomplish. I have children, Sarah. You need to find a man that will give you all that fresh—not used up and already worn."

"It seems as though you've given this a lot of thought." She swallowed the annoying little lump in her throat; and she could not understand why her legs suddenly felt cut off from the rest of her body.

Finally, he smiled. "I have. Every time I've seen you stare at me as if I'm the evil Jack springing out of the box. When you knock at my door and tremble so hard I wonder if I'm going to have to pick you up off the floor." He paused from studying her hands to glance at her face. "Or like now, when your cheeks color for no good reason, or when I come up behind you and you jump as if you're about to yell rape."

"That was a normal reaction," she answered weakly. "You scared me..."

He put a finger across her lips. "Shh, like what you're doing now. You've suspended breathing, waiting for my reaction, for my next move—fearing it and expecting it at the same time. Sitting on a fence is no way to live your life, pretty lady," he added, sliding his thumb gently across her mouth before dropping his hand back down to his fork. He kept his eyes downcast, waiting for the written message he knew she would read in them to disappear.

"Well, it's none of your business how I live my life," she scorned him, spent and fragile, unhinged by the notion that he could read her this well.

"Exactly," he smiled. "And if you agree that the same is true for me, then we can have a truce and be friends—deal?"

She nodded, unable to utter a single word. She picked at her food for the next couple of minutes. It suddenly tasted bland and all the same.

"We've had some exciting developments in your case," Julian finally added, dishing out Pot au Feu for both of them. "I should've mentioned for you to talk to me if you were unable to reach Cox. I forgot—I've been running around these past few days…"

"You're not the one who is following me, are you? Is there even someone who is?"

"There always is. But you're right. It's not always me. Don't worry," he added, noticing the disappointment on her face. "The two people I've chosen are trustworthy and very capable."

"So what have you discovered that is so exciting?" she asked, nibbling at her vegetables.

"Ray is in Paris." Julian waited for his words to sink in.

"Detective Cox is in Paris? Why? What can he possibly hope to find there?"

wishes, the French authorities got into the picture. Ray's coming back on Monday. We'll know more about it then."

Sarah was awestruck. "My parents—murdered…all these years of missing them." The restaurant had filled up fast since they had first arrived. Sarah lowered her voice. "Julian, my faith has always helped me to be strong. It has," she acquiesced when she could not read his eyes. "It has seen me through lonely years, hopeless situations…There was the…balm of certain inevitability when believing my parents were taken from me by an act of God. But to think that they were cheated out of their life—that I was robbed of my family because of someone's greed…"

He handed her a tissue. *Please don't cry, Sarah. I couldn't take it if you did.*

"Thank you." She wiped her eyes and blew her nose.

"I don't think you should get upset until you hear from Ray. It might not be the reason."

"But you're saying that the French authorities…"

"And the Swiss police," Julian added.

"That they've suspected a man-made accident?"

"They know it's a man-made accident. They just don't know why. The answer would lead them, no doubt, to the possible culprit."

"All these years…"

"Listen, when Ray comes back next week, he's likely to have a few questions for you. He might ask you to remember the earlier years, when your grandfather was still alive—the names of any friends Clément Goddard might have had, any family members not readily known."

He even knew her grandfather's first name, Sarah thought, longing for his shoulder to lean on. "Could it be someone at the law firm?"

"We can't know that until we know more about who stands to gain." Julian reached for her hands. "I'll go with you if you like—to Ray's office, to lend support."

Sarah had never seen him so attentive. It was tempting to take him up on his offer, to let go the strain and relax on his double-vested strength. But she remembered his earlier request that she not bother with him anymore—that she forget the intimate moments they had shared.

"That's okay. I'll be all right on my own. That's part of my life business you think I should lay elsewhere, remember?"

Gone was the solicitous kind light in Julian's eyes. She saw him recoil as he reclaimed his hands to slink back in his chair.

A storm began brewing in his dark eyes as he glared at her from across the table. A muscled twitched in his jaw. And if he chose to say nothing, and not rise while dragging her out of there to leave immediately, it was out of respect for her precarious emotional state—for the hurt that was preventing her from realizing how foolish and callous those last few words were. She could not know, he thought. She just did not realize how much he loved her.

CHAPTER SIX

"No buts, ifs and don'ts. I'm going with you, Sarah."

Mark was adamant. He stood by her small living room window in a cashmere grey herringbone jacket over black matching pants, looking like a model from some weekly, filling her apartment with the alluring male scent of Calvin Klein.

Sarah gazed at him, hands on hips, ready to protest. In a way he reminded her of Julian—same pluck, same determination many would call stubbornness. She sighed, a small part of her glad he was going to be there for moral support. "Okay. Since I can't talk you out of it."

Mark smiled and walked up to her, nuzzling her cheek. "If I'd known that pig-headedness was all it took to climb the stairs to the tower, I would have gathered my princess a long time ago." He smiled and took her into his arms.

Sarah returned his hug. She felt comfortable and safe inside Marks' arms.

He pulled back to stare into her eyes, then gently, so as not to frighten her, he bent to kiss her lips. Sarah returned his kiss. It was light and gentle, non-threatening; but when Mark increased the pressure, attempting to part her lips with his tongue, she propped her hands against his chest, pushing him away to avert her face.

The episode with Julian was still so vivid, too predominant for her to trust her senses to another sensuous kiss. In reality, the Julian incident was still so fresh that the heart in her cringed to be in Mark's arms, as though she was cheating on Julian. This is ridiculous, she chided herself, embarrassed to the hilt.

"I'm sorry, Mark. I guess I'm just not ready…"

"Hey! Don't say another word. I know you have a lot on your mind. I'm patient, my beauty," he murmured in her ear. "I'll wait for as long as you want me to."

On the ride over to the police station, Sarah pondered that this may have been what Julian was trying to say, the day they had lunch. If they were going to have normalcy in their lives, they had to forget about their one-night torrid affair and move on. There was no movement in the replay of that sad Saturday night. On the flip side of that event stood Mark, gallantly waiting for her to let him in. It was up to her to take his hand and lead him through.

She relaxed in the fine leather seat, reached for his hand, and gave him the brightest smile in her repertoire. He squeezed her hand before riveting his attention on parking the car.

Once at the precinct, climbing up to the second floor office of Ray Cox, Mark sensed Sarah's nervousness. "Poor baby," he told her, kissing her forehead and strapping an arm around her waist. "I'll be here for you, every step of the way. You have nothing to worry about."

She smiled up at him as they arrived in front of Detective Cox's office. "What would I do without you," she told him, nestling in a little closer. Mark glued his eyes to hers as he stretched to open the door—both of them walking through it together.

"Looky, looky; they're busy peckin' each other's faces." Sarah was the first to regain her senses as she searched the office for the feminine voice behind the words. Then she noticed Julian.

Julian! Sarah could not believe he was there. A punch in the stomach would have given her just as much difficulty to breathe.

"Pleased to meet you, Detective Cox. I'm Julian's brother, Mark."

Julian was standing against the back wall, looking foreboding in tight jeans and a black leather jacket. He cocked his head toward her in a guise of politeness, but she could tell by the little muscle in his bottom jaw and the darkness of his onyx eyes that he was angry with her. What had she done now?

The tall girl standing next to him was staring at her with open defiance. She was the girl she had seen in his room that night—the girl responsible for that goofy remark when they entered. Sarah had summed her up correctly. She was her height, stylish, with short dark curls and immense dark eyes. Her mouth was full, heart-shaped and ruby-red. Not only was she also leaning against the back wall, she was standing as close to Julian as she possibly could. She was leggy, wearing an extremely short tight skirt and an even smaller red Halter-top.

"Thank you for coming, Miss Miller." This with a shy smile from burly Ray Cox who wore his suit like a big round-shouldered bear. Even the hand he extended was broad and covered with hair.

"See, someone thanks her for comin'. All you do is force me here at the point of your fist!" The tall dark-eyed beauty elbowed Julian as she spoke, giving him a crooked smile. She was chewing gum or eating candy, moistening her lips with a hungry tongue every so often.

Julian's lip barely curled. He kept staring at Sarah, a hard look in his eyes.

"What's everybody doing here?" Mark asked, directing his question to Julian.

"I'm helping Ray with the case. This raven beauty

is Renata Varone. She's also helping Ray with the case."

"Are you a police officer, Miss Varone?" Mark wanted to know.

"Nah. And I'm not doin' this for Ray. I'm here providin' my friend Julie with R & R. He got me out of a bummer way back when. Taught me how to fend. I owe him." She shrugged her right shoulder, giving Mark a petulant stare.

"Renny has a black belt in Karate. She knows the city; she knows the ropes. She's been…investigating for me," Julian supplied to explain Renny's cryptic phrase.

"I see," Mark answered.

Sarah was grateful to Mark for asking all the questions she was hesitant to form.

"R & R?" Mark continued.

Renata smiled at him brightly and boldly putting the onus on popping her gum. "Yeah! Run and Rat. I run people down, then I rat on 'em." She laughed; a quick, contagious laugh that made Sarah smile.

"Have you been running me down, Miss Varone?" Sarah just had to ask.

Brown eyes warred with green eyes; and where green eyes sparked the mesh, dark ones were quick to ignite.

"Yeah, I have. Only 'cause I was told to. Peepin' on broads ain't my usual. But what Julie tells me to do…I do."

She spread her hand on Julian's chest as if to claim him as property, and Sarah bit her bottom lip not to laugh.

Julian read the humor in Sarah's eyes. He bent to Renny's ear and whispered something that made her flick her shoulder at him angrily, snort and swing her head in the opposite direction.

"I wanted you to meet Renny, Sarah. She's been kind enough to keep an eye out for you, and on any suspicious marauder she might deem worth noting."

"I am pleased to meet you, Renny." Sarah advanced and extended her hand. "I am very grateful for your diligence. I know it's probably not easy to do."

Renny smiled at her. She checked Julian, then when he nodded surreptitiously, she approached Sarah and shook her hand. "You're welcome. You're easy to run—it's nothin'." She shrugged. "Just so you know, I won't be rattin' on you."

Sarah nodded and shook her hand, noting the girl's long red nails. She was obviously utterly devoted to Julian and Sarah wondered fleetingly if there was anything other than a teacher-student relationship between the two.

Mark tugged on Sarah to sit beside him.

Julian sat on the edge of Ray's desk, and Renny stayed at the back, as quiet as a mouse. It was obvious Julian had asked her to be silent.

"I just don't see why so many of us need be present here when this is Miss Miller's personal, private affairs, Detective Cox." Mark insisted they be alone.

Julian got up and strode to the back of Sarah's chair. Unexpectedly he began rubbing her shoulders. His motion was firm, soothing, and Sarah didn't readily object. "We're here to lend our support." Julian's thumbs worked circular miracles on the knots in Sarah's nape. "We're working on the case and this is the best way we know of cutting through the red tape, get the information first hand—not rehashed at some second sitting."

Sarah's head began moving from side to side, gently feeling the pressure lift from tired aching muscles. She suddenly remembered Julian working on her back as she had lain face down on his bed, his hands rummaging through the tense muscles in the small of her back. He had tickled her senseless with dozens of hungry kisses all the way down her spine. The thought jerked her upright.

"What are you doing?" Mark asked, suddenly concerned. "Sarah doesn't like that."

"How do you know?" Julian asked, continuing the rubdown.

"It's okay, Mark. I'm sure it's simply Julian's way of trying to make me feel better." Sarah smiled at Mark to reassure him.

"Good girl," Julian added, patting her neck and moving away to his perch on the desk.

Still, inwardly she was angry with him. How dare he just arbitrarily decide to rekindle what she had taken so long to numb? This, after suggesting that they move on and forget what had happened between them. Men, she sighed. Were they all so thoughtless?

Mark threw Julian an angry glare before turning toward Cox. "So, what have you got?"

"A lot, but then again, still not quite what we want," he answered cryptically. "The French authorities were glad to see me there. They've been trying to solve this one for twenty years." Cox got up from his chair and began pacing from his desk to the door. "They showed me the files on this one, Julian. They were thick. Boxes of them. They followed every lead in the book. Spent many years trying to tie in the leads they had to a French politician who died on that train. The authorities were breathing down their necks…"

"I don't understand." Sarah asked him. "Why didn't they look into my grandfather's activities?"

"Maybe they did. There was nothing on file, though. I guess there was no reason. Your mother was due to inherit, yes. But your grandfather still held the purse strings when she died. The old man didn't suspect anything—case closed."

"What kind of…fortune are we talking about here?" Mark suddenly asked.

"We don't know—not officially. They're still working on an injunction to get the will and its stipulations released. It's a different system in France—the Napoleonic code."

"Can't I instruct them to hand me the information?" Sarah asked.

"Uh, uh. Not until you're twenty-five. You'll have that right on your birthday."

"Not officially? Do you have some vague idea?" Mark

persisted.

Detective Ray Cox looked at each of them, assessed that there was no one in the immediate vicinity outside his office. "What I heard from one of the partners of the firm St-Cloud, Cuinard, Laffé…we're looking at a couple of hundred million."

Sarah drew a sharp breath. "Francs?"

"Nope. American dollars."

"Oh my god!" Sarah was visibly shaken.

"Are you sure? Can that be right? Gees! That's a lot of money." Mark was shaking his head.

"What could that old man have possibly been up to in order to rake in that kind of dough?" Julian wanted to know.

"His estate owns a couple of vineyards north of Lyon. Big ones, it seems. Apparently it all started when he began to help prominent people escape the war, from 1941 to 1944. They repaid his kindness with paintings and works of art. He would sell them every now and then and invest the cash. But in the seventies, when the value of lost masters skyrocketed—their words not mine—the firm managing his accounts scored big."

"Could it be this firm is worried about Sarah reaching twenty-five and placing the money elsewhere?" Mark asked.

"Don't know. If it is, then they could be responsible for that train crash as well."

Julian peeked at Sarah to see how she was holding up. He got up and stood behind her. "Could this be why they're so reluctant to release the information?"

"They're within their right. Protecting the privacy issue. Any other firm would do the same. Still…"

Julian grabbed a chair, yanked it to him and straddled it to face Sarah, to better talk to her. "Sarah, remember what I asked you, the other day when we had lunch?"

She nodded, feeling Marks questioning eyes on her. She had omitted telling him of that episode.

"Do you know of anyone who might stand to gain from your grandfather's will?"

"I don't, Julian. It's not my father or any of his brothers; my grandfather never liked my father any more than he had to." She closed her eyes trying to recall some family lore. "I vaguely remember my grandfather saying that his mother—my great-grandmother, was not his mother. At the time, I thought he was being facetious. He rambled on as he got older. But he repeated it several times. I remember visiting my American cousins when I was thirteen. I had come with a nanny. My Aunt Karen told Nicky that I looked like my great-grandmother on my mother's side. She had pulled out a picture and looking at the photo, I remember telling her that she wasn't the one. The one I had seen in a photo on the mantle in Grandfather's room. That's when she had confirmed that my real great grandmother had died in childbirth and that my great grandfather had remarried."

"But you told me that your grandfather was an only child," Julian told her.

"I assumed he was. He never mentioned any other children by his step-mother."

Cox and Julian looked at each other briefly.

"That could be our first lead," Cox said.

"That doesn't make any sense," Sarah told them. "If my grandfather had siblings somewhere, they would have gotten it all when my grandfather died."

"Not if he died intestate, or, having made a will that left everything to his granddaughter. If this was the case, the only way they could inherit would be by getting rid of... you," Mark told her, squeezing her hand.

"I would've known if he had half-siblings. He would have told me."

"Not if he wanted nothing to do with them," Mark added.

"They would be old by now. Why go to all that trouble?"

"It might not be a direct half-brother or sister, Sarah," Julian told her softly. "It might be a descendant—a child of these people."

"A child would have been too young to be responsible for the train crash twenty years ago."

"Not necessarily. A half-cousin could have been your mother's age—even older. You once said that your grandfather and grandmother did not have your mother until their late thirties..."

"My grandmother was in her late thirties; my grandfather was forty-eight."

"When did he pass away?" Mark asked.

"Eleven years ago. That's when I came for a visit to America. Aunt Karen had some of my mother's things. She showed me pictures." Sarah was pensive. "Why not then? Why wait until I'm so close to inheriting?"

"Tricky," Ray Cox added. "All good questions that mean we've got some serious investigating ahead of us. If we can get our hands on your grandfather's will, it might clear up a lot of stuff. But for now, we can't count on it."

"Julie, can I say somethin'?"

All heads turned to face Renny, who had stood in the corner as quiet as a wallflower for the last hour.

"Go ahead, sweetie."

Sarah winced to hear Julian call this other woman by such an endearing term.

Renny smiled at him. "Let go of the little punk—the dirty-blond hitter. I'll run him down. Bet ya, he leads me right to baddy."

Cox and Julian stared at each other, wide-eyed. "Why didn't I think of that?" exclaimed Cox.

"That's my girl, Renny." Julian rose, walking toward her, and he patted the back of her head.

He was pleased with her, Sarah thought. All that was missing was the little treat one hands a pet for good behavior. Such condescension, she rued, not a little bit envious.

"You realize," said Sarah, "that if he slips through anyone's fingers he'll be right on my doorstep."

"Not to mention," added Mark, "he may have been a one-time hitter. Whoever hired him is liable to stay away—seek fresh game."

Cox shook his head. "We went through his last six-months of bank records with a fine-tooth comb. He received no large sums of money, no small deposits—nothing. He's living off a small job as a delivery boy. He shares a room with an older man. We think they might be a couple. If someone had hired him for a one-timer, they would've paid him by now."

"It's a place to start," Julian told them. "Maybe we should keep tabs on both the hitter and his older partner.

"Sounds like a plan," Cox concluded. "I'll start the paperwork to get him released."

In the corridor downstairs, Mark was leading Sarah to the door when Renny called out to them. Caught up and out of breath, she pulled Sarah to the side.

"What's the meaning of this?" Mark asked, none too politely.

"You get. This is girl talk. We don't need you interferin'." Renny was gripping Sarah's arm.

"I'll meet you out in the car, Mark." Sarah smiled at him. "Go, it's okay. I won't be long."

"Where's Julian?" Sarah asked her, surprised to see Renny further than two feet away from the man she obviously adored.

"He's up there with the Cox fella." She burst a little bubble from her gum. "I just wanted you to know that I'm going to take real good care o' ya. Don't be scared or anythin'."

Sarah was genuinely touched. "Thank you, Renny. That's really nice of you."

"I'm doin' it for Julie. He's got the hots for you somethin' fierce."

Sarah shook her head checking to make sure that Mark had gone.

Renny laughed. "That's why I asked the chump to leave. I would watch my step 'round that fancy pants brother of his. He's nothin' but a loafer—a taker," she added when she sensed that Sarah didn't understand. "Julie just keeps him on. He's his brother—promised his mom."

"Why do you say that about Julian—where I'm concerned, I mean. Did he say anything to you?"

Renny shook her black curls, wet her lips and gave Sarah a knowing smile. "He'd never do that. He's too gentlemanly." Renny ran her fingers in Sarah's hair, fluffing it up on top. "You got nice hair. Julie likes that." She ran the back of her hand against the skin of Sarah's bare arm. "Soft skin too. I know Julie likes that." She laughed. Then she reverted to being serious. "He doesn't sleep anymore. Doesn't like his bed—so I kind' a figured somethin' happened there." Renny smiled and flicked Sarah's tell-tale red cheeks. "When you saw me there the other night it was 'cause I wanted to see who you were. He'd told me to get out of sight when he heard you knock. Still doesn't know you saw me. Later he drove me downtown, then he slept over." She waited for effect.

Sarah's expression grew somber—delighting Renny, proving that she was right. "Don't worry, I got a spare room. Jules is a one-woman man. For a while, before he knocked-up and married Marissa, I thought he'd turned queer or somethin'." Renny laughed. "But even when he was hung up on her, I never seen him like this."

"Why are you telling me this?" Sarah asked in a small voice.

"Because you gotta be nicer to him, beauty. You can't go mooching around with his brother in front of him. I mean, Julie is the sweetest gentlest man I know. But he's got a temper—know what I mean? One day he might explode or somethin'. Cut him some slack."

Sarah nodded. "Thanks for the advice, Renny. I'll be more careful."

"You know, hon, for everything he's doin' for you, it wouldn't kill you to give him some." She smacked her lips together and gave Sarah the crooked smile. "More of the same—whatever that was, he appreciated."

She turned and left Sarah standing there, legs weak and ears ringing. Now she knew why she never heard noise in the room next to hers. She pressed her hand against the cold marble wall to steady herself and took deep breaths to calm her nerves. She thought of Julian rubbing her shoulders tonight, in front of his brother even, and only now realized how overwhelming his urge to touch her must have been.

Sarah gathered her strength to focus her thoughts back to the ride home with Mark, and promised herself to be more attentive to Julian's feelings in the future. As for the last advice Miss Renny Varone had just handed her, there was no considering it without losing her sanity.

CHAPTER SEVEN

John and Karen Miller, their daughter Nicky and her boyfriend Leonard, Professor Frank Minsk and his wife Bella, Mark Spinner and his niece Melissa were seated in the front rows of section A of Alice Tully Hall, attending the 15th appearance of the Quartet-In-Residence of the Chamber Music Society.

The Society was celebrating two of its newest and most prominent artists, pianist Daniel Radcliff and cellist Sarah Miller. The concert was to open with Beethoven's String Quartet in A Major—one of his earliest and sunniest compositions, followed by Mendelssohn's String Quartet in A Minor. The program would later unfurl to an accompanied cello performance by Miss Miller interpreting Frantz Schubert's Der Tod Und Das Madchen—Death And The Maiden. Mr. Radcliff's accompanied interpretation of Beethoven's Appassionata Sonata would be next, preceding the grand finale.

The group had arrived ninety minutes earlier at the Hall, dressed in grand pomp, to partake of a scheduled wine tasting festivity to lead off the concert. All of them were genuinely relaxed and ready to enjoy the musical extravaganza ahead of them.

Sarah had donned a green taffeta dress fitted with a low décolleté satin bustier, and wore her hair in a loose intricate French braid interspersed with satin ribbons. Nicky held her breath when she first saw her.

"It's no wonder Julian fell in love with you when he saw you in concert, Sarah," she whispered. "You look like some wood nymph—a musical fairy. I'm so proud of you, sweetie."

"Thank you, Nicky. Speaking of Julian, did you see him anywhere?"

Nicky shook her head, pleating her nose. "I'm sure he's here. Bella told me he asked Frank for his tickets. I just think he's patrolling the place—making sure it's safe."

"Maybe you're right."

"Mark's here. Front and center," Nicky smiled.

Sarah nodded. She knew. She just didn't think it was the time or place to tell Nicky that ever since Renny had daubed Mark in a less than flattering light that day at the police station, Sarah didn't find him as charming as she once had. He was kind and gentle; but she had noticed that his amiable manners seemed aimed at scoring him points rather than boosting genuine friendship. She had found Renny extremely astute and had asked Julian to invite her to tonight's concert.

Once everyone was seated and there remained only a hush of anticipation, the Maestro came on stage to vivid applauses, saluted the audience briefly, then initiated the orchestra's commencement notes with a wave of his baton. Slowly, as the lights dimmed, the music wafted upward and through the acoustics until it filled every living space. Gleefully, Beethoven's allegro quartet rebounded playfully, sprinkling gaiety, never resting, always running, enthralling young and old with its vivacious tempo.

Up in boxes B, left and right, were two silent figures eyeing their surroundings through powerful binoculars, searching for any suspicious movement in the silence and stillness of the audience below.

Julian had pleaded with Sarah not to perform this evening. She was a riveted target, he had argued. But he knew she would not disappoint her peers or the promoters counting on her virtuoso performance, or the patrons who had paid dearly to come and see the new darlings of the Society. He admired her aplomb to continue living on her terms and not cower before a nameless enemy.

He was worried, though. This darkness and reverberation of sound echoing from everywhere at once were perfect foils for a foe with no face.

Renny was in the box to the right, and both were patrolling the audience in the first three sections. Another sharp-eyed friend—an arms and weapons master stood at the back in the loges. A plain-clothes policeman stood at every entrance, and despite this state of readiness, a sense of foreboding still crept up Julian's back. He flexed his shoulders feeling a cramp coming on. Either the tuxedo was too tight or he wasn't used to wearing one.

When the soft hue of spotlights came to illuminate Sarah's figure down on stage, signifying her turn to solo, it took all of Julian's will not to park his binoculars on the woman he loved. She resembled a soft apparition as she glided into her piece, the rest of the orchestra providing gentle background. He remembered that it was a difficult piece to play. He had never been fond of the tragic-sounding chords. But she rendered it beautifully, poignantly capturing the desperate essence and wild tempo of the Fugue in D Minor. In a way, the musical arrangement reminded him of their cryptic, seething affair—dramatic and jumbled, and wincing from all edges.

He breathed a sigh of relief for Sarah's safety. She was nearing the end of her performance and…he detected unusual movement in box A to his left, a glimmer of some kind. He couldn't see from his angle.

"Renny," he whispered into the walky-talky. "Check out box A to my left—in front of you. There's an awful lot of movement there. Do you have a better view?"

"Yeah! They're movin' all right. I take that back, our guy's a loner."

"How do you know it's a man?"

MELODY INTERRUPTED

"Don't see no skin. Got to be a suit. Even he's naked, don't think any dame would come solo to a shindig like this."

Julian couldn't help smiling. Renny knew how to break down common sense to its smallest denominator.

"Julie, that's a telescope. The guy's mounting a telescope. He's a shooter. I'm headed there to cut him off."

"No. Guard the exit. You'll never make it. I'm going to run him down."

As Julian ran out of his booth, he mowed some man down, stepped over the head of another, and stirred up enough commotion for the shooter in the forward box to know he needed to be deft and quick with his lethal volley.

Julian was way past caring whether he was seen or heard. A bullet traveled faster than the beat of a heart—no matter how far it raced.

Sarah rose, as invited to do so by the Orchestra's conductor, and approached the edge of the stage bathed in light. She curtsied and, as she did, her instrument's bow she had nervously carried with her fell and threatened to drop over the edge. Delicately she crouched to retrieve it. When she rose from her curtsy, she sensed commotion in the booth closest to her and heard members of the orchestra scramble back stage.

The curtain fell behind her and the audience, unaware of any disturbance, rendered their gratitude continuing their thunderous applauses. Slowly, the front rows' fervent began to stand; then, like the ripple effect from a giant wave, the one thousand-plus crowd gave Sarah a standing ovation. After long minutes and many flashes of cameras, the stage attendants handed her the symbolic bouquet of flowers and escorted her off stage through the right wing.

Sarah was winded, but elated. She was glad there would be a small entr'acte before the last two pieces. Putting down her bouquet, she noticed a stretcher laid out and gasped as she saw Daniel Radcliff being given IV by the on-site paramedics. She ran toward the stretcher, clawed her way through and knelt on the ground beside Daniel's still body trying to elicit some response from him.

He opened his eyes and smiled lightly. "You were great," he muttered. "Please tell them I'm sorry. I won't be able to play the Sonata."

"You're going to be fine, Daniel. I will tell them you'll be back. Don't worry."

She glanced at the paramedic, fighting back the tears, looking for confirmation of her statement. The young man nodded saying it was a bullet in the upper right shoulder. It was a bleeder but they had him stabilized. They moved Sarah out of the way, and Carmine, the tall second violinist of their quartet, steadied her with an arm around her waist. Quickly, they hoisted the patient to the back alley's emergency exit and into a waiting ambulance.

With Carmine's help, Sarah collapsed into a nearby chair. "What happened?" she asked the art director.

"We don't know. Apparently there was a shot that no

one heard because of the noise of the applause. We saw Daniel fall off his bench. When we picked him up, we saw the blood. We'll have to wait for the outcome of the investigation before we know why." Philip De Pang sounded winded and mechanical, as if he'd just run up a hill to discover he was lost. He was in shock, and Sarah told Carmine to fetch the paramedics for him as well. Her legs refused to support her.

Other co-performers were devastated, and Lydia volunteered to forgo her place in the violin section to go with Daniel to the hospital.

The assistant art director went on stage and announced that due to unforeseen illness, Daniel Radcliff would not be playing this evening. The audience sighed, genuinely disappointed. He continued, saying that after the entr'acte only one piece would be played.

From somewhere, Julian found her. "Sarah," he muttered, pale and out of breath. He saw the blood-soaked stain on the skirt of her dress and knew seconds of sheer panic.

She stared at his eyes, shaking her head. "It was Daniel. He's been shot, Julian; they say he's going to be all right. But there was so much blood. I must have knelt in it."

Letting out an enormous sigh of relief, Julian scooped her up in his arms. For precious minutes, he just held her, trying to stop her from shivering, from crying.

"Oh, my God!" Julian rained kisses on her cheek, in her ear, in the braids of her hair. "I thought I'd lost you."

"I should have listened, Julian." She muffled the words

out, pressing herself against his chest. "I should have listened to you. Daniel would not be hurt if I had."

"Don't be silly, Sarah. You're not responsible for the random actions of a madman. Whatever made you bend—just in time to avoid that bullet?"

She moved in his arms to look at his face. "I don't know. I've practiced these few steps hundreds of times. Nerves maybe—I clutched my bow and didn't stow it like I normally do. Even forgot I had it with me when I waved and took a bow. Then it fell and I just crouched to pick it up...I felt like such a klutz...and now poor Daniel..." She choked, unable to finish her sentence.

"It's okay," he soothed her. "I heard your performance." He tried to distract her.

She sniffed. "Were you there?"

He nodded. "It was beautiful, Sarah. I am so proud of you."

She smiled. "I was so nervous knowing you were out there somewhere—listening—watching me. All I could think of was trying to find where you were..."

He gave her a half smile and suddenly, a frown on his face, he began searching her eyes. The message he detected there drove him to the edge. If what he read in her upturned face, in the loving green eyes she flashed on him was true, it was tantamount to a punch in the gut. He moaned, the sensation driving him to the brink. He had to be sure. "Say it plainly," he whispered. "No more half-truths—please?" he begged.

"Sarah!" She heard her name called from several directions at once. Renny was running up from the right; escorted by a guard, Nicky and her aunt and uncle were arriving from the left. Mark followed the procession, pushing and shoving the others in an attempt to get there first.

Sarah smiled at them; she did nothing to extricate herself from Julian's arms. Proudly Julian held his grip on her and did not loosen it even when Mark arrived and gave them both a strange look.

"Are you okay?" Mark asked, suddenly sobered by the stain of blood on her dress.

She nodded and politely slid out of Julian's arms. "I'm fine, everyone. There's been an accident. Daniel Radcliff..."

"The police think it might be a stray bullet from a sniper's gun," Julian intervened, wanting this to be the official version for now.

There were audible sighs. Frank Minsk knew the boy well, as did Bella. Nicky and Mark were the only ones who suspected otherwise, and Nicky paled when she received confirmation from the raised eyebrows and the look in Julian's eyes.

Sarah gave Mark a warm hug to reassure him, moved to hug Nicky and her parents, then thanked Renny as their eyes met.

"Hey! I'm the one who's thankful. You're takin' my advice, I see." She indicated Julian and didn't care who knew it.

Sarah smiled shyly, averting her eyes. She knew she had left Julian in the lurch. But she could not give him the simple answer he requested. She didn't know what she felt just now, or how much of this overwhelming desire to be buried in his arms was due to shock.

"Your performance was magnificent." Professor Minsk told her when he approached to shake her hands.

"I even cried," Bella said, still dabbing her eyes with a tissue.

No one else mentioned the incident that had her dress stained with Daniel's blood. They took Julian's statement at face value.

"I don't want you to play again," Julian admonished.

"There's no need to be so bossy about it," she scolded him. She pointed to her dress. "I would have to change if I was, and there's no time."

"Good. I'll drive you back."

"I'll drive her back, bro. She's had just about enough of you for awhile, right Sarah?" Mark was daring her to argue, not understanding that she had no fight left in her whatsoever.

Julian knew. He nodded, then left just as quickly as he had arrived.

Sarah watched him leave, Renny at his side. The last dregs of will that remained in her wondered why he was so curt with her. Why he had not bothered asserting his elder's right to drive her home. It was his house. He was younger brother's keeper. Sir Galahad had better things to do, she thought, her irritation with him resurfacing again.

"Did you catch the guy?" Julian asked Detective Cox on his way out.

Ray Cox gave Julian a long, disgusted stare.

"Don't tell me, he ran…"

"Vanished, is a better term."

"Doesn't surprise me. When I got to box A, he'd just scrammed. And when I looked for a way out, I had a choice of five different directions—it was worse than playing musical chairs. That's when I found my way to Sarah as fast as I could. I was worried that seeing he'd missed might bring him back stage."

"Good call," Renny affirmed.

"Well, we've got the telescope and the rifle. It's off to the lab. I doubt if we'll lift any prints off them. If he left them behind, it's because they're clean."

"Hey, the jerk had no choice. Who knows?" Renny added.

"Go home, kiddo," Julian told Renny.

"You comin' later?" Renny batted her eyelashes at him; she wanted to know if she should make up the spare bed for him.

Julian shook his head. "No. I'm going to face my big, bad demons. Got to do it sometime," he smiled.

"I got a feeling you'll get lucky tonight," Renny added with a wink.

"Come by tomorrow early," Ray Cox told Julian. "Frenchies are faxing me important information in the early hours of the morning."

"I've got a staff meeting tomorrow morning. I've been putting it off for a while. I'll call you around lunch, Ray."

When Julian got home, the house was dark. The nanny had left around seven and Carla, the babysitter, had gone once Mark had arrived. Mark had not parked his car in its usual place, and Julian wondered why he had suddenly decided to take up the whole right side of the drive.

He climbed the stairs two by two and tiptoed up to the attic.

Melissa had just gotten undressed and was getting ready for bed. "Hi, Daddy," she smiled, plopping her arms around his neck. "Isn't Sarah wonderful?"

Julian smiled. "She is, muffin, she is. I take it you enjoyed her performance?"

Melissa nodded with wide eyes, as only a seven-year-old could muster, and asked, "Is that man going to be all right, Daddy?"

"Absolutely, sweetie. He's going to be fine."

"That's what Uncle Mark said."

"And…isn't that enough?"

"Well, you know Uncle Mark, Daddy. He'll often tell us exactly what we want to hear."

Julian tickled her and made her giggle; then he gave

her a huge raspberry-kiss at the base of her neck. His little girl was as wise and precocious as an old hoot.

"Daddy! Stop that. You're getting my neck all wet." Melissa wiped herself with the collar of her pajamas.

"And you're nothing but a little old lady," he told her mockingly. "Keep up the long face and you'll be washed up by the time you're ten."

"Like you're too old for Sarah?"

Julian stared at her, her spontaneity robbing him of a better reply. "Is this what Sarah told you?"

"No, silly. Sarah doesn't think you're too old for her. Uncle Mark does. Is it true?"

"Age, little princess, is something like hair style or eye color. You like it long or short. You have them blue or brown. It's a question of taste."

"I think I understand," she added. "Some people prefer the life they had as children. They like to be with young people. Some people prefer life to be more grown up. They want to be with people who have experience."

Julian laughed and shook his head. "And where did you get such a fat head," he told her, amazed by her perspicacity.

"It comes from growing up without a mother," she told him, knowing how to tug at his heartstrings. "If you want me to lighten up, you're going to have to find me a new mother," she admonished seriously. "Brad feels the same way."

"Well! I guess I'm outvoted, outranked and outnumbered. I'll keep my eyes open," he told her as he scooped her up in his arms to put her to bed.

"Goodnight," he said from the door. Just before closing it he asked, "Any special request?" Julian smiled, giving her his sidelong glance with the cocked eyebrow.

Melissa giggled, her little face under the double layer of sheet and blanket. "Yes," she told him, laughter in her pretty voice—muffled by the covers. "Someone like Sarah. The more like her, the better." Again Melissa gave him a shy bout of giggles.

"Well then, my little friend, that is a pretty tall order. I'll have to see what I can do." It was Julian's turn to laugh lightly. He closed her door softly.

Down the corridor he passed Sarah's bedroom door. He stopped in front of it, his hand poised to knock. He hesitated. This is silly, he told himself. Why would he let a sheet of plywood and a little drywall stop him from talking to the woman he loved? That's all that stood between them for now. But tomorrow would turn the corner and the whole gamut of taboos would plunk their heads in the way of their happiness. His brother Mark, Sarah's youth, the fact that she was still terrified of him were just a few of the kinks that needed smoothing.

He sighed and walked away. Entering his room, he stared at the bed he hadn't slept in since Sarah had laid there beside him. He approached it like a cowboy about to mount an untamed bronco, sitting tentatively on the edge, smoothing the ruffled blanket. He wondered where Sarah was at this very minute.

Sarah was soaking in the tub. She had put lots of peach-scented bubble bath in the water to relax. Slowly, the hot vapors had begun to lift some of the day's tension from her body. It had taken her an hour to unwind, to forget how close she had come to losing her life. It was difficult to excise Daniel's painful smile from her mind and to forget how weak he had appeared on that stretcher. Even as she let go of the sight of all that blood, there was still the matter of Julian's urgent plea; that she express her feelings for him clearly.

The people pressing against her had saved her from having to answer him. Now there was nothing to prevent the question from bouncing around from head to heart. She had yet to discover why he irritated her at times, why she frequently needed to lash out at him. For instance, she hated the way Julian had succumbed to his brother, nonchalantly giving in to Mark's whim to take her home. He had gone from pride of holding her in his arms to indifferently tossing her to the care of someone else.

She had not been comfortable in the car with Mark. She had thanked the stars that Melissa had been there also. Mark had played the taciturn martyr all the way home. He was sulking. Had he noticed the raw tension between her and Julian? That was the only explanation for his stubborn silence. Once in the house, he had dismissed her with a peck on the cheek and half a smile before driving the sitter home.

A noise suddenly roused Sarah from her torpor. She

sat up in the bath. She heard the water running in the other bathroom—Julian's bathroom. She listened intently. He was taking a shower. Her heart skipped and skidded at the thought that he had decided to sleep in his room tonight.

She waited for him to stop the water, then impishly she turned on her tap full blast. After closing it, she waited to gauge if he had heard it. Would he knock on her door now that he knew she was awake?

Just then she flashed on Renny, remembering when she had asked her to cut Julian some slack. She felt immediate remorse for having tempted fate, and prayed he had not heard or noticed because she still could not give him an answer. One thing she did know. She no longer feared him.

Julian considered turning the handle to the communicating door to Sarah's room. He did not want to wake her or frighten her. Just stare at her as she slept. He remembered the latch and thought she had most likely locked the door. On the other hand, if he knocked, she would open. Then he would be face to face with the woman he most wanted to hold in his arms for the rest of his life. Would he be able to control himself? Or would he be risking a repeat performance of the Saturday night they had spent together?

He doubled back instead, opting for sleep and peace of mind.

But sleep took a long time to come. So, when he heard Sarah calling his name, he knew he had to be dreaming.

"Julian..." She walked over to the bed. "Julian." She shook him a little.

This did the trick. "Sarah?" His voice was groggy. He sat up on one elbow. "Is anything wrong? What time is it?" He glanced at his watch and a few seconds passed before he could focus enough to see the time. "It's 2:00 in the morning, sweetheart. Are you all right?"

She closed her eyes for the tenderness welling up inside her. Even as he slept, his thoughts of her were gentle. But then she cringed, thinking that this was crazy. She had no right disturbing what little peace he had.

"Forget it, Julian. It's silly." She started walking away.

"Sarah," he voiced peremptorily. "Talk to me?" he asked, his voice softer this time.

She turned to face him. "It's just that I keep having this dream..." She wrung her hands nervously.

"Come," he told her, moving aside, patting the empty place in the bed beside him. "Tell me about your dream."

She came to the edge of the bed. She put out of her mind the memory that he slept in the buff and climbed in, staying as close to the side as she could.

He draped the sheet and blanket over her. Even in the pale light of the moon, he could tell she was terrified.

"Someone climbs the trellis outside my window, enters the room and points a gun to my head. It goes off and then I'm walking in all that blood..." Sarah stretched out beside him. "...my blood."

Delicately he sidled up to her, scooping her up in his arms so she could lean her head against his chest.

She didn't object. She was willing and malleable.

"There," he told her as he cuddled her and wrapped his arms around her. "You don't have to be afraid, Sarah. No one's going to get past me. I can promise you that." He kissed her forehead, and as he looked down at her face, she was already fast asleep.

Well, looked like he had gotten his wish. He had wanted to see her sleep. He sighed, wondering how he was ever going to find sleep himself; especially when the soft scent of her jammed up his senses.

"Goodnight, sweet Sarah," he whispered.

CHAPTER EIGHT

Sarah opened her eyes and took a few minutes to remember where she was. The room's view was an eastern exposure and the early sun poured through the tall windows. She guessed Julian had forgotten to close the shutters. Glancing his way, she saw him lying on his side, his back to her, the sheet and blanket down to his knees. She shouldn't, she knew, but she couldn't help staring at him. He looked like Adonis—so taut and powerfully built. Unable to resist, she bent, stealthily brushing her lips on the back of his bare head.

Delicately, so as not to wake him, she eased out of bed and lightly stepped toward her bedroom door.

"Good morning, Sarah!"

She jumped out of her skin having gotten only halfway there. She turned to look at him and saw that he still had his back to her. He had not budged.

"I thought you were sleeping," she told him. "I didn't mean to wake you," she spoke in a hushed tone. "Go back to sleep. It's only 6:30."

"I wasn't sleeping," he continued without moving, "…heightened senses…martial arts."

"You were sleeping soundly last night," she countered, a smile in her voice.

He clutched sheet and blanket and yanked them waist-high before turning to look at her. "You came in around 2:00 something. You walked halfway to the bed, hesitated and turned back then called my name a couple of times. When you noticed that this didn't work, you shook me a little."

"How…?"

"I heard you, Sarah. Just didn't think it was real—thought I was dreaming."

He sat up in bed, rubbing his face with his hands. Then he deliberately rubbed over the part of his head she had just kissed. He smiled when he saw her cheeks color. "This was nice, by the way. A very small token, mind you, to show all of your appreciation—but it was nice," he smiled.

"Didn't know you were keeping tabs."

A wicked smile crossed his face. "You'd better get out of here before I decide the tab needs to be settled now."

She smiled, not biting the bait, continuing toward her door.

"Sarah?"

Grasping the handle, she turned.

"You headed down to the Center this morning?"

She nodded. "And to the hospital. I want to see Daniel."

"I'd call first. They might have released him already. Just—be careful...what you say. I wouldn't tell people you were the intended target. We're not even sure of that yet."

"I won't say. Nicky's the only one who knows. Mark never made the connection, I'm sure. Do you think it could be just a coincidence?"

He shrugged. "Does seem strange that the person who was bent on having your death look like an accident would suddenly go all out with a professional shooter in the midst of a crowd of a thousand people."

She nodded. She liked the little ray of hope that said the accident might be a random one. "Thanks...for everything, Julian."

"Anytime," he smiled slyly. "I am available tonight should you need expert cuddling."

She turned and crossed over to the safety of her room. She leaned for a few minutes against the door she had just closed, finally fully breathing. She smiled, a contended, elated smile. She had just found the answer to her question—the root of her irascibility toward Julian. It stemmed from lack of trust. She no longer feared him and now, she trusted him—completely. Two out of three was good. She breathed contentedly. Two out of three was very good.

Julian had just adjourned his two-hour staff meeting. He was in the office of his block-size Manhattan gym—the largest of his three establishments. He was harried, tired and grumpy from lack of sleep. This morning he was plain bad company, and pouring over the books did nothing to restore his foul mood.

"Hey! When you gonna can that bozo Mickey?" A dirty haggard old man dressed in a straw hat and a long shredded coat had just let himself into Julian's office, barely shuffling his feet off the floor. "He's a low-life who thinks he's better than me. Treats me like the shit under his two-bit gumshoes, like I'm some kind of bum o' the street or somethin'."

"Hi, Arty. Don't bust my chops this morning. I don't have time to hear your sobs. Besides, you are a bum off the street."

Arty Maiz sat down in front of him. "Yeah! Well, just 'cause I happen to retain sleepin' accommodations in the alley don't mean I ought' a get less respect than the next guy. All I'm askin' is for you to talk to the guy. Jiminy! He sucks up to that weasel brother o' yours. You'd think he'd have more sense than to asswipe a moocher."

"I told you before, Arty. Don't badmouth my brother. He can take care of himself. The kid brought in 150 gees last year from that fancy-pants job of his."

Arty Maiz laughed. "150 gees! I got three times that much—stashed away."

Julian looked up from his books. You couldn't have

paid Arty any amount of money to sit in a bath or stand in a shower. He hated being around people or being trapped inside four walls. He was untamable—Julian had long since given up trying to make him fit. "You're a crazy old man, Arty. What are you doing with all that dough? Say a truck hits you tomorrow. That paper's just going to rot somewhere."

The old man hesitated. "Then maybe it won't. Maybe I'll tell someone. Then they'll find it. I mean, someone could know that it's in a blimp bag down by the pier—shed number nine—buried under them bricks…" He gave Julian a toothless grin. "Big chunk's yours, anyway."

Julian shook his head and returned to the books and spreadsheet on his computer. "So, what have you got?"

"Nothin'—nada—zip. No contract. Never was."

Julian heaved a sigh, pushing himself away from his desk. "You're slipping, old timer. There's a contract. I know."

"Hey! I went to the docks on this one. Had to pay Skipper money. He loads off the Nina and Santa-Maria, handles all the commercial paper on them contracts…"

"Look, you don't have to tell me who writes it up, or where he works or what he does. I want to know who is holding."

"That's it. Nobody."

"Are you telling me that no one in the city has a contract out to kill this girl?" Julian handed him a picture of Sarah.

"Jules! I swear on Lincoln's grave. If there was somethin' written up, Skipper'd know about it."

"So maybe it's from out of town."

"Can't be. Every contract, whether it comes out of Detroit, Vegas, or anywhere else, they know to pass it through Skipper's boss and his merry men. If they didn't, they'd be fish bait in the harbor inside forty-eight hours. These things get around. And, Jules, a contract on a classy dame like this…" He lifted his shoulders in a dramatic gesture. "It's rare. That'd be like…matter for chatter. Know what I mean?"

Julian was silent. "So, that could mean the hit was engineered from outside the country…"

"Can't help you there. Jules, who's the beautiful babe? She as hot as she looks?"

Julian cracked half a smile. "Yeah! You could say that."

"Then, what's she doin' with your loser brother? They was out here this morning when I came in."

He suddenly had Julian's undivided attention. "Sarah was here?" He sprung up from his chair, walked to the door and yelled out to Mickey in the outer office.

"Boss," Mickey came running. "Relax. What's the urgency? Use the intercom or somethin'. You're disturbing the patrons." He eyed Arty with disgust. "If it's about being nice to this stiff…"

"You don't have to be nice. Who you are, that's your business. But you can be polite. Every idiot in the world can manage polite. Think you can?"

Mickey, short and stocky, scuffed the heel of his shoe

against the floor. "Yeah, I can." He threw Arty a scornful glance.

Julian turned toward Arty. "Thanks, man. Go by the club tonight. Darren will have your cash."

Arty laughed and shuffled out.

"Mickey? Why didn't you tell me my brother and...his girl came by this morning?"

"You were in the meetin'. You said you didn't want to be disturbed."

"Next time this girl comes looking for me...she's priority."

"But Julian, she wadn't lookin' for ya. Just hooked up to your brother—you know, he had his arm around her...he seemed nervous to talk to you or somethin'."

"Thanks, Mickey."

"Don't mention it."

He left Julian standing at the door to his office, deep in thought. Maybe that's why he was in such a rotten mood. Even after the closeness Sarah and he had shared yesterday, she had still avoided telling him how she felt. Even after he had bared his heart to her. There it was. He had just said it to Mickey. She didn't have to be nice—pretend to feel what she didn't feel—just had to be polite. She was being polite. No answer could be the polite form of the one answer he did not want to hear.

The sigh he heaved was loaded. It did nothing to relieve the pain in his gut. Still, the facts were plain. She had been here this morning, with Mark, and had not even asked to see him.

Julian walked into his office to answer the phone. "Julian."

"Hey! Don't sound so gloomy. We've got great news."

"Hi, Ray. I was just hurrying to finish up. I'm on my way to see you; can it keep?"

"Sure. Just don't be long. You'll be pleasantly surprised."

"Yeah. Sure, man."

Julian closed the door to his office and returned to his books. He needed to balance the figures on his computer's spreadsheet. The accountant was complaining about the data being overdue. He had to be there early tomorrow morning to pick up the books. At least, thought Julian, as much as he hated it and considered himself poor at it, the math took up the bigger part of his brain, giving him some respite from longing for Sarah, a yearning that was putting him through hell.

When Julian got to Ray Cox's office, it was past 3:00. He was tired, and just lifting his legs up those stairs felt like he was dragging five-pound weights.

He was told, Cox was alone in his office. He knocked and let himself in.

"Sorry I'm so late, Ray. Hope you have coffee. I could sure use some about now."

"I always have coffee. Sergeants from other departments tank here." He indicated the slew of empty decanters along the credenza wall. He poured Julian a mug from a fresh pot.

"What's so exciting?"

"Your friend, Sarah and her beau—Mister your brother—came by here early this morning. They sauntered down to your place after. I guess you couldn't see them."

"My manager never even told me they were there. But, that's another story. What's up?" Julian could see that Ray's morning euphoria had simmered down. He had already shared it with the others and he worried that Ray was just going to provide him with filler.

"A humongous break is what's up. We got the stats on the will and all its provisions. That's all we needed." Ray smiled, the excitement over the luck he had experienced resurfacing in a jiffy.

Julian looked at the legal papers and letters written in French that Ray handed him. "You'll have to translate." He shook his head. "I've been in the books all day. No way am I even going to touch this."

"Julian, these papers state unequivocally that Goddard had two stepbrothers from his father's second wife. One of them is named Simon, he's sixty-five; and the other is Joseph, he's five years older. In this letter, dated September 1965, Goddard stipulates that he agrees to lease them the land and the vineyards he owns, north of Lyon, for no less than ninety-nine years. They can work them, reap the profits from the sale of the wine and manage them as they see fit. In other words, he retains nothing else but the deed on these vineyards."

"Big gesture!"

"Not really. At the time, the taxes on the land cost more than what the vineyards were bringing in. Goddard did this to rid himself of the trouble—not to mention the drain on his cash flow."

"What happened?"

"As the story goes, the vineyards prospered. Simon and Joe raised families of sons and as their progeny grew, so did the business. Thirty years later, it's worth a small fortune. Meanwhile, the impressive extensive art collection owned by our friend Clément had stopped being a cash drain. Collectors sought his pieces and they became worth an absolute fortune. They filled Sotheby's and Christie's. The rest you know."

"But technically the vineyards are still his, right?"

"His assets total close to the half billion mark—in good old American currency," Ray told him excitedly. "That's without the vineyards."

"But he still owns them?"

"Yes of course, the Estate still owns the vineyards."

"Wow! So Sarah knows this?"

Ray nodded. "Told her this morning."

"What's the deal? You seem to think you've solved this."

"Let's just say, it was solved for us." He smiled, shaking his head. "The truth is that as long as the old man was alive, or as long as the law firm managed his assets and that they weren't turned over to any of his direct heirs, the lease remained. Now that Miss Miller's about to turn twenty-five, the addendum to the lease stipulates that she can reclaim the vineyards for..." Ray took a couple of pencils on his desk to strum an imitation drum roll..."one dollar."

"What! What are you talking about? Who in their right frickin mind would accept a crazy arrangement like that?"

"Ah! At the time, the vineyards weren't worth much. And the grandfather wanted to leave something for his children and his children's children should he die broke...or having accumulated debt. At the time, he didn't know about the value of those paintings."

"The poor chumps probably signed this agreement thinking they were the luckiest bastards alive and that they'd cross that bridge when they came to it, I guess."

"Something like that. Oh! That ex-fiancé of hers, Serge Courcelles? We think he might be a distant cousin. Probably the son of the younger brother, Simon. He may have taken his mother's name as camouflage. We're still looking into it."

"How did he ever expect to get away with this?"

"Losing a hundred and fifty million dollar business to the tune of a dollar will tend to have people pull crazy stunts."

"But they couldn't have been responsible for that train wreck...They had nothing to gain by killing Sarah's parents."

"Now you're thinking like a cop."

"So what you're saying is that the French authorities are back to square one?"

"Too right. That's why Goddard never complained. First he was grief stricken; then, there was nothing to complain about."

"Sarah will be relieved. She couldn't stand the thought that her parents were murdered by some money-hungry schemer."

"I know. She told me."

"So, one of the brothers is responsible for the attempts on her life. Maybe both of them are." Julian was animated. Finally, he foresaw a little light at the end of the tunnel.

"We don't know that for a fact. Actually, one of their lawyers is under investigation—information they weaseled out of the ex-boyfriend. They've been busy over there."

"What about last night's shooter?"

"Turns out he wasn't aiming at Sarah."

Ray nodded vigorously, faced with Julian's stunned expression. "The boy is fine. But the boy's father came to police headquarters this morning. He asked us for protection. He's an accountant with an interesting list of clients. One of them is a Long Island gang of thugs—looking for revenge. We're checking into legit ways to pick up their fearless leader—some two-bit punk with too much pimp money."

"Are you sure?"

"The bullet's trajectory, the timing—they weren't aiming at Sarah. Luckily, you were fast on the shooter's tail. A couple of inches made all the difference. Odds are he wouldn't have missed had you not been there."

Julian was more than stunned. He was shocked. "What about the hitter, the one you released the other day?"

"He couldn't have done it. A trolley fished him out of the water, early this morning. The body appeared to have been submerged for at least twenty-four hours."

Julian sat back in his chair, a look of knowing dawning on his brow. He remembered Arty's words. It was incredible. The underground faction was quick, lucid and well deserving of its name—organized.

"What, you know who did this?"

"It's another story—later," Julian told him. "So, the only lead to the culprit behind this is Serge's testimonial…"

"Yep. And apparently he's singing like a lark. So, they'll have the perpetrator behind bars before the week's end. Oh! And Miss Miller's a smart cookie. She contacted her lawyer in France. He's putting an agreement together that is going to lift the dollar stipulation from the lease once she turns twenty-five. She thinks it's fair and that the vineyards should revert to the Goddard brothers. Between you and me, with the inheritance she'll be receiving, she won't need the wine."

"Still, that sort of rewards the bad guy."

"Nah. Once they identify the chump, he'll be out of business. France has a fairly strict code of ethics for dealing with would-be murderers."

"Don't we all."

So that was it. A neatly wrapped up, perfect little bundle. Julian raised his hands, signifying it was all over...

"Didn't I tell you it was exciting?" Ray Cox was jubilant. He couldn't have been happier had he personally materialized the stroke of events that cleared up the mess. "I mean, these are the cases we work for. The ones we can touch, feel and solve."

"That we do."

"You and I both know that once a case goes unsolved for a couple of months, it goes stale and eventually gets colder than dry ice, until no one wants to put time and money into it any longer. Our poor pathetic little precinct is not like television, where most crimes get solved in the last fifteen minutes of the movie. We don't get those kinds of breaks."

"That we don't."

"What's up with you, Julian? You sound like you're not happy about this."

"Of course I am. Who wouldn't be?"

But as Julian drove home, he wondered what would happen now. While he was ecstatic at not having to worry about Sarah's life anymore, he was moody about not having to worry about Sarah. He no longer had the mandate to watch over her like some guardian angel. He no longer had any excuse to afford her his whole attention. Did he need one? If she had expressed that she wanted to be with him it would be different. But she had obviously spent the day with Mark and never even asked about him.

When he arrived at the house, he noticed Mark's car parked in the drive. He hopped out of his jeep and walked toward the door, his legs cramped and as heavy as two wooden pillars. As he entered the foyer, he heard Sarah's laughter coming from the second floor. He closed his eyes and remembered their last night together. Now she would no longer require his expert cuddling.

"Hey, Julian," Mark addressed him from the top of the stairs. "I'm just helping Sarah get her stuff."

"Hi, Julian," Sarah smiled at him, a strange look in her eyes.

Julian nodded. He could not do small talk. Especially when he was seething with rancor. Had he opened his mouth, they would have known it immediately.

"Did you see Ray?" Mark asked.

"Just left him. Congratulations, Sarah. Everything turned out for the best after all." He stared at her, willing her to find the hidden meaning in his words.

She nodded. "Mark was kind enough to offer to help me pack. I thought it would be better than disturbing you." Slowly, she walked down the stairs to stop not one foot away from where he stood. "You've been extremely kind to me, Julian. You've turned your life upside down for…my cause." She raised her chin, trying not to let too much emotion show. "There is no way I can ever properly thank you."

A couple of ways come to mind. Julian shook his head slowly, a wry look on his face.

"And I...I don't wish to be indebted to you. I would rather we be friends..."

There was the polite answer he had hoped never to hear. "True friendship and proper politeness make for strange bedfellows, Sarah, as unfortunately sometimes people do also."

He had hit home. Her smile disappeared. Was he referring to himself as a true friend and to her as prim and proper? Was he saying that their lying together had been a mistake? To be a dominant man and have to fold...She held her tongue. Her opinion had drastically changed concerning Julian. She could not imagine her life without his friendship. She extended her hand. "Well, I think we made perfect bedfellows," she whispered her eyes wide and shy.

He cracked a half-smile. "We did, didn't we?" He pushed her hand aside and gathered her up in his arms. "I'll be the best friend you ever had," he murmured as he kissed her on the lips.

Sarah returned his kiss, and she sighed from his unexpected shiver.

CHAPTER NINE

"So that's it? That's how you left it with him?" Nicky felt gypped. Where was the romance, the happy-ever-after ending? "Now you're back in your one-room, poorly lit, boring apartment."

"None too soon. If I'd stayed there one more night… plus, my geranium died."

"Well, I'm not surprised. There's not enough light in that apartment," Nicky answered nonchalantly. Veering her full attention to her cousin, she told her, "Sarah, I think you're the clueless princess."

"Why do I sense an insult coming on?"

"First night you meet Julian, turns out he's irresistible." They were seated at the deli on Amsterdam. Nicky was up to her third cup of espresso and she was wired and not understanding the attraction Julian had on Sarah. "He's so irresistible that you end up living at his house where you constantly worry about his presence on the other side of the door...long for it, fear it. You curl up in the man's arms—one whole night in order to find the blessed sleep of the innocent...Sarah, it should be evident even to you that you're in love with this man. It's pathetically clear to me."

"Well, it's not clear to me. Turns out, I don't know what love is. I thought I did when I was engaged to Serge. Look where that brought me."

"That's normal. I could have told you that you didn't care one zip for that guy." Nicky shook her head. "A Frenchman who can't get your pants down passed your hips." Nicky clucked at her with the tip of her tongue.

Sarah rolled her eyes heavenward and smiled. Nicky had so many tricks up her sleeve. "Love is not about sex. It's about two people sharing dreams together. It's about spending the rest of your life with your soul mate. Look at all the things Mark and I have in common. We always have topics to discuss; we're both artists who enjoy making music."

"Talk, talk, talk. That feels more like friendship than true love."

"Love is not lust, and lust is not love."

"Convenient. Whatever happened to you discovering Marks' insincerity; the one pointed out to you by Renny? You told me that you now found him to be nothing but a big fat phony."

Sarah sighed. She remembered the sensation she had

felt that evening. "Nobody's perfect. At least he respects me. Nicky," Sarah placed a hand on hers, "when I'm around Julian, all I think about is…"

"…him giving it to you?"

"Nicky, you're shameless…" She was right, thought Sarah dejectedly. And when she wasn't thinking along those lines, she was thinking about her giving it to him. "That's just it, Nicky. When I'm around Julian, my mind is always cluttered with all these images…as though I'm in the gutter and can't ever emerge from it. I have these urges…Look, all I know is that I lose sight of everything and everyone when I am around him. I lose sight of myself—what I'm supposed to do, who I am…it scares me."

"I could diet on that."

"I become weak—and I'm never weak."

"I hear you. Still, if I had to choose…" Nicky's eyes drifted off. "Maybe I should ask him out…would you mind if I gave him a shot. After all, he is alone."

"You're incorrigible, Nicky," Sarah sighed.

"You're not jealous—are you?"

Nicky was up to something, Sarah thought as she eyed her suspiciously. "What about Leonard?"

"He's okay, I guess. But I can talk shop with any of my classmates. That's why people have them—friends, I mean. But Julian is entirely yummy. He's out of this world yummy," she sighed.

Sarah grew silent. She didn't want to be caught up in

Nicky's game, and yet part of her still worried about her cousin making good her threat.

As for Nicky, she knew there was nothing she could say that would change Sarah's mind. She would have to come to that realization herself—hopefully with a little psychological push.

"Anyway," Sarah added, "Julian made it very clear the day we had lunch…"

"When was this? You never told me the two of you had lunch."

Sarah smiled shaking her head when faced with Nicky's insatiable curiosity. "People eat, you know. That day, we happened to eat lunch together…"

"Where?"

"Does it matter? At the Café des Artistes…"

"What? A hunk takes you out to lunch in one of the swankiest shops in town and you pleasantly neglect to tell me about it?" Nicky motioned with her hand for Sarah to put out. "I want all the juicy details."

Patiently, Sarah recounted the circumstances leading up to the luncheon date and the lunch that followed.

"So basically, you were flirting with him and he called you on it. Ha!"

"A friendly smile doesn't constitute flirting…"

"Oh! Come on, Sarah. This is me; I know you. If it's the smile I think it is—the one where your eyes get into the act and silently emit this homing signal that bleeps, 'here I am, vulnerable, frail and so available'."

Sarah laughed at the expression on her face. "I don't do that. I've never even been close to…to that face you've just made."

"Of course not. You do a much better rendition." Nicky ordered a pastry to soak up some of that coffee.

"Anyway, as I was saying, as you now know, he made it very clear that I was to forget about that Saturday evening and move on."

"That's not what he said."

Sarah laughed. "You, who weren't there, are going to tell me what Julian said."

"Of course. Psych 101; first thing they taught us—how to speak Martian. You're just missing the Venusian translation."

Sarah laughed, waiting in spite of herself for Nicky's explanation.

"What he really said was, 'Sarah, please don't flirt with me if you don't intend taking it to the next level.' Tut-tut," Nicky forestalled her. "I'm working here. Now, what he said next was, 'I have more experience than a younger guy and I have a ready-made family just waiting to love you'. And finally, yet importantly, the very pivotal phrase, 'I think we should forget about that Saturday night—since it was such a poor way to begin our relationship—for you, not for me, and move on with our lives, TOGETHER.' That's what Julian said."

Sarah laughed, trying to picture Nicky's words coming

out of Julian's mouth. "Men are not that complex, Nicky. You know they're not."

"Sweetie, that's the whole point. Men are just like us. They have the same fears—did she like the way I performed. Has she had better. In our language, it simply translates as, will he still respect me in the morning—identical—just different words."

Sarah was silent. It would explain why he had pounced on her that night at the recital when he had caught an unguarded emotion in her eyes, why he was hounding her ever since about confiding her true feelings.

"That's why when you told him you wanted to be friends, that was the Venusian equivalent to the Martian kiss of death."

"Why can't we be friends?"

"Because he's in love with you, Sarah."

"So, when he kissed me and told me he was going to be the best friend I ever had—translated, that means what exactly?"

"That he accepts your kiss of death, that he's going to avoid you like the plague, and that you're never going to see him again."

Sarah sat back into her chair, totally deflated. She did not want to believe it, but somehow Nicky always made a lot of sense. Why would she be wrong now, simply because she didn't like what she was hearing? "Pray to god you're wrong, Nicky. I so hope you're wrong."

"Why? Because you can't harbor for even an hour the thought of never seeing Julian again?"

Not for a minute. Sarah's eyes reflected her torment. She nodded slowly.

"Can you say the same for Mark?"

In a practical logical world, Sarah was dating Mark while continuing to mix it up with Julian—as a friend of course. Sarah did not answer.

Nicky saw she was troubled. "Hey! Forget what I said, Sarah. I was just jerking you to prove a point. I'm sure you'll see lots of Julian—especially if you hang with Mark. He's family. He'll have to be around. Off the subject, how about you and Mark coming to supper on Friday night? I have the house to myself. The folks are gone to Aunt Sophie's for the weekend."

"I thought Leonard had group on Friday nights."

"Not this one. And, we can wear off some of those calories by going dancing after."

"That sounds like fun." Sarah had lost her spark. The interpretation Nicky had given her concerning Julian's words bothered her. Could she have misread him?

"Stop thinking about Julian. Have you counted the number of hours you spend in contemplation of this man you are not in love with?"

Sarah gave her a wry smile. "You're right. I can't get him out of my mind. It's like an obsession or something."

"Everything but the L word," Nicky muttered between

clenched teeth.

"You know, even if what you said is true—about the language and the interpretation…there is still something bothering me."

"I know. Julian bothers you—a lot." Nicky gave her an exasperated look.

"When he looks at me…I don't know, I mean, he manages to make me feel inept. Nicky, the man makes me blush. I haven't done that since I was ten years old. What does that tell you? It tells me it's not a comfortable feeling."

"The cat and mouse syndrome."

"Yes, exactly! Thank you. That's exactly how I feel."

"Only to Julian, you're the cat. This lovely, alluring, purring kitten that has a paw on his…"

"Don't say it!" Sarah interrupted her guessing where she was headed. "You're unbelievable!" she laughed. "I can't believe you were going there."

Nicky laughed also. "Well maybe the metaphor is a bit much. Nevertheless, Julian does think you're the one toying with him, jostling him back and forth, and his condescension stems from insecurity. I mean, guys don't blush—when threatened, they attack."

Sarah nodded. She had to admit that Nicky's construal revealed a side to Julian she had not envisaged. "Anyway, the poor man's ears must be ringing. We have to stop talking about him—because I've got to stop thinking about him. Okay. Where do you want to go dancing?"

"Just leave it to me. I know the perfect place."

Julian was finishing his training routine. He was in the process of dismissing his class of eight bodybuilders when his manager Tony walked into the room.

"Jules, there's a lady out here wants to see you. I told her you were busy. She says it's important."

Julian strapped a towel around his neck, wiped the sweat off his face and had to ask. "Is she a tall blond looker?"

"No. She's a looker, but more the petite blue-eyed brunette type."

For a couple of seconds he tried to figure whom he knew that fit that description. "Take her business card. Tell her to come back later."

"Sure thing."

But as Tony turned to go deliver his message, the brunette who had followed him there tried to push her way through.

"Hey missy, hold on a minute. You can't go in there." Tony laughed as he held Nicky by the shoulders barring her way and refusing to let her in.

Julian recognized her and intervened. "It's okay, Tony. I know this one. Let her through."

"Be my guest," Tony bowed and let her pass. Nicky adjusted her sweater and sleeves. This Tony is a bully, she thought.

Julian had his back to her, putting weights away and

wiping down machines.

Nicky swallowed a lump in her throat suddenly understanding the full gist of what Sarah had been trying to tell her. This man was gorgeous. His tank top was short, small and cut halfway up his back while his baggy cotton pants hung flimsily on his hips. She had the full view of his back—the rounded shoulders, the long neck and the smooth shaven head. When he bent, she saw the small of his back exposed, as muscular as the rest of him.

Her resolve weakened, and she who was strength incarnate felt a trembling sensation invade her lower limps. Had her legs been stronger, she would have run, not walked out of there. This tall broad man oozed charisma and sex appeal. She had clearly underestimated his power, and Sarah's resistance, for that matter.

By now, her silence had Julian intrigued; and still with his back to her, he cocked his head sideways in her direction.

"What's this about?"

Ooh! He was curt and short. Not at all the reception she had imagined. Nicky took a deep breath and steeled herself to accomplish what she had set out to do.

"I need to talk to you about Sarah." There, it was out.

Julian turned toward her, tightening the cord at the waist of his pants. His look was quizzical yet foreboding. Nicky promised herself never to make light of Sarah's plight again. He had the most inscrutable eyes that bore right through a person. As though he knew secrets about you that, even you dared not discover.

"Is she all right?"

"Yes, of course. But I have something to discuss with you." Why was she fighting to find her words?

"I don't have much time, Miss…"

"It's Miller. Nicky Miller. I'm Sarah's cousin. We met at the station…then the house, then…"

"I remember," he said simply, a strange smile on his lips. Seeing she was not going to add anything until he had agreed to listen, he smiled, and raising his eyebrows, extending his hand, he offered her a seat on one of the benches in the fish-bowl room. People coming and going were obviously paying attention to their every move.

"Isn't there anywhere more private we can talk?"

"There is," he answered guardedly. "But then you would have to sit and wait in my office while I took a shower."

"I can do that," she answered, using the same tone.

He gave her a mocking half-smile, and without another word, preceded her out of the exercise room.

As tall as he was, Nicky noticed he was barefoot as she trailed him to a door on the second floor.

Julian opened the way to a large airy office. The couches were leather and the desk was a simple glass-topped table. "Make yourself comfortable," he told her as he walked to an adjacent door, turned on the light so that Nicky saw it was a huge gleaming white bathroom. Without closing the door, he threw the towel he had around his neck in a nearby hamper and took off his top.

When Nicky realized he was striping in front of her, she moved to the part of the couch that didn't allow her to see him naked and showering behind glass doors. She fanned herself with one of the magazines strewn on the table in front of her. This man was hot, sizzling hot. There were no innuendoes about it. He was the real bad boy—no pretence, no fuss and no muss. She mentally tried to picture him at the recital, the proud nurturing way he had held Sarah in his arms and had trouble believing this was the same man. She had missed how very formidable he was. Her thoughts returned to that Saturday night Sarah had tearfully described to her. Had this man stopped making love to her mid-stream, she too would have begged him—no, paid him a king's ransom to continue.

He came out of the bathroom wearing a loose robe, still barefoot. Julian smiled when he noticed the far corner she had picked to sit in. "You can come and sit here at the bar, I don't bite."

Oh! I beg to differ. She got up and walked over to take a seat on a stool in front of what resembled a small kitchen counter.

Julian was gathering produce from a cupboard and a corner refrigerator, preparing ingredients he was dumping into a huge commercial blender sitting on the counter. "I'm making a whey shake. Would you like one?" he asked, a mocking lilt to his tone.

"No, thank you."

He retrieved another glass from the cupboard, filled it half with orange juice, half with Perrier water. "Here, Nicky," he told her in a much softer voice. "This simple concoction is meant to restore courage to the lionhearted." His eyes gazed into hers and she experienced the inadequacy Sarah had spoken of, tenfold.

"So," he interrupted his sentence with the noise of his machine. "What's this important matter concerning Sarah that you so urgently need to discuss with me?" He filled his glass and indicated for her to follow him to the couch.

Once comfortably seated, she almost lost her nerve when faced with a riveting stare and a brow furrowed with curiosity. She opted for the direct approach. She figured toying with this man's emotions might be dangerous, but no more so than fidgeting under his unnerving glare. "I know about you and Sarah," she stated simply, waiting for his reaction.

Slowly, his lips curled into one long Cheshire smile. He turned in his seat on the couch to properly face her. "Do you?"

"Sarah is not only my cousin, she's my best friend. We have no secrets from each other." She saw a muscle twitch in his jaw, and the forced smile he had donned faded completely.

"What has she told you?" His tone was measured and, she recognized, deceptively soft.

"Everything." And for the first time in her young life,

Nicky worried about another person's reaction. He was not taking this well. His eyes were dark and foreboding. If they had been weapons, she would be struck down in her prime—lifeless on his carpeted floor.

"Sarah does not strike me as the type to gossip." He had paled, clearly livid.

"She's not. She didn't go into details. But she was very upset, Julian. I'm the closest friend she knew to confide in."

"I see. So what do you want from me—financial... help?"

When the meaning of his words became clear, Nicky spit her drink back into her glass so as not to choke on it as she burst out laughing. She shook her head, unable to stop. When she did, she took a deep breath to apologize. "Oh, my god! She's right, Julian. You are a big bully."

Unexpectedly, he smiled from ear to ear relieving some of the tension between them. "She said that?"

"Not in so many words—soo many words—Julian, she can't stop talking about you. She is so in love with you, it hurts me that neither of you knows this." There, she had said it.

Once more, the smile was gone and the sullenness was back. He rose to walk to the counter to put his glass down, keeping his back to her. "She knows how I feel, Nicky."

"Not really, she doesn't. I mean, she heard your words and understands that you long for her—probably the same way she longs for you; but she doesn't believe you really love her."

He turned to face her. "I couldn't have been any plainer. I'd give my life for her, and she knows that too."

"I'm not going to argue with you. It's pointless—just as it was trying to talk some sense into her. You two are made for each other but speak different languages. Like the other night, when you cavalierly allowed your brother to take her home."

"She was in no mood to endure a scene. Mark's next option would have been to put her through the humiliating task of choosing. I know him. I thought it best to spare her, to leave."

"To spare her, or yourself? I'm sorry," she added quickly. "That was uncalled for. But I'll have you know that she was miserable. Mark was a double-digit ditz to her all the way home. She was just grateful your daughter was there as a buffer."

"I'll kill him," Julian muttered under his breath, making tight fists.

"That's the other thing that scares her—creating a rift between the two of you. Anyway, you're so bent on doing what's best for her that you're shoving her right out of your life—to her detriment, I might add. And she's too proud to recognize this." Nicky was talking more to herself. "What a mess."

"Why are you here?" Julian asked, looking tired all of a sudden.

"I'm here to help my cousin. I don't want her to end up

with Mark. I don't think they're right for each other. Worse, she's not in love with him."

Julian sat back down in the matching chair facing the sofa. Without looking at Nicky, he admitted. "I've tried everything. I've tried releasing her, telling her to stay away...so she wouldn't feel trapped..."

"...reverse psychology—no good on Sarah."

He threw her a hard sidelong glance. "I've tried cajoling her, begging her..."

"...frantic, needy—misread that as a desperate stab at sex," Nicky shrugged.

"What are you," Julian harped, "an amateur shrink?"

"Third-year psychology student," she inched in carefully, her face stretching into a comical apology.

Julian could not help smiling.

"And I wouldn't use the bully approach anymore—she just deems it as having been...ravished," she finished lamely, realizing too late, she had overstepped her boundaries.

Once again Julian was furious enough that his eyes made her physically recoil into the sofa.

"God! They've already taught you to be mindless and useless—like most shrinks."

"I have a plan if you want to hear it," she added haughtily.

For a long time, Julian just stared at her, up and down, trying to gauge whether she was sincere or whether she had an ulterior motive.

"I'm having her and Mark over for supper on Friday night. Then we're going out dancing. She thinks my boyfriend Leonard will be the fourth party. But…you could be my date for the evening, then we would switch. I'd keep Mark busy while you entertained Sarah."

Julian stared at her intently until she could no longer support his gaze and lowered her eyes. Then deliberately, slowly, he walked over to the sofa. He sat down beside her, cupped her chin and flicked her head to face him. "I don't think you want me as your date, little Nicky—I am liable to ravish you," he sneered, emphasizing the word. "I don't think making Sarah jealous is the answer either," he added, still holding her face in his hands. "She would see right through that. She knows I will only make love to her. Unless your real target is my brother Mark?"

Nicky rolled her eyes to the side and burst out laughing, disengaging her face from his grasp. "Yeah, right! As if… Do you have a better idea?"

Julian sat back, his eyes staring in the distance. "Actually, I do. I might just have a workable solution."

CHAPTER TEN

"More lasagna, Sarah?"

"I can't squeeze in another bite. It was delicious. You'll have to give me that recipe."

"It's a one-pan wonder. You just layer anything you like." Nicky sucked the tomato sauce off her index finger. "Just have to make sure you use lots of mozz, and there you have it. What about you, Leo?"

"I'll have some more," Leonard smiled stuffing away the last bite to make room on his plate.

For the intellectual type, Sarah thought he was a big eater. "I can't understand what came over Mark," Sarah commented, her eyes pensive as she stared at Nicky going from the counter to the table.

Nicky sat back down to another plateful of pasta and a piece of garlic bread. "That is strange. He usually follows you around like a wayward puppy. What was his excuse again?"

"It wasn't so much what he said but the way he said it."

"Sometimes," interjected Leonard, swilling his food in his mouth, "there is no subterfuge—an excuse is simply an explanatory conduit to a valid reason."

"We know, Leonard, we know." Nicky patted his hand. Turning her attention to Sarah, she asked. "What were his exact words?"

Sarah shrugged. "That he had a family emergency; that he needed to go away for a few days and that he'd be back on Tuesday. That we would talk then…"

"You're right, Sarah. The boy is strange." Nicky answered.

"It's the way he added that we would talk…it sounded gloomy."

"Didn't you say he is a music agent?" Leonard asked. Neither Nicky nor Sarah bothered answering. "Well perhaps he had to settle a score with an out-of-town client," Leonard added anyway.

Sarah thought that Leonard's explanation made sense. What didn't make sense, she countered, was the three of them going to the 10:00 p.m. party at the Fifty-one Club. Sarah felt like the odd man out, the buggy's fifth wheel.

When they got there, Leonard made sure to walk between them, looping both ladies' arms with his.

"See, Sarah?" Nicky told her, all excited. "Aren't you

glad you came? Now we can be a ménage-à-trois."

Sarah gave her a quizzical mocked-frightened sidelong glance, wild eyes edged toward their partner in the middle, and Nicky burst out laughing.

"Yes," answered Leonard who had missed Sarah's funny facial expression. "I feel like one of those gangsters about to bounce a moll on each knee," he grinned.

It was Sarah's turn to burst out laughing. When her eyes became accustomed to the dimness of her surroundings, Sarah surveyed her short strapless black sheath and felt a tad overdressed. Many had on their party garb, which for the women meant bejeweled and as naked as possible. One young woman was dancing and gyrating to the DJ's clever mix wearing nothing but a clingy sheer dress covering nothing more than would a see-through stocking. The music was deftly loud, the lights flickered in psychedelic shades, and waitresses in bikini tops and skimpy aprons were scurrying about the club in five-inch heels.

Leonard placed a hundred dollar bill in a huge bouncer's hand with special instructions.

"Sarah," yelled Nicky, "I hope that girl doesn't get a run in her stocking."

Sarah smiled and nodded, noticing she wasn't the only one skimpily dressed. One young woman's dress was so low-cut down her back they could see the top of her jewel-studded thong. As for Nicky, she wore a black faux-fur bra and a skimpy thin wrap-around skirt. She'd obviously been here before, thought Sarah, and had opted to adopt the area's easy mores. The men were dressed in suits and jackets while many of them favored ties.

The bouncer brought them to a special closed-off seating section where the music was less overbearing and the tables catered mostly to couples taking full advantage of the primitive beats and secluded atmosphere.

"Do you come here often, Nicky?" Sarah wanted to know once they were seated next to the table of a couple taking their petting very seriously.

Nicky smiled. "Whenever I want to get my guy in the mood. Naked chicks turn him on." Nicky nibbled on Leonard's ear, and he turned and kissed her on the mouth. Once again Sarah wondered why she had agreed to come. She sighed, thinking that this was going to be a long couple of hours.

They could see the bar from where they sat and Leonard waved bills in the air to attract the attention of a tray-carrying waitress. But when the girl behind the bar saw him, she left her island behind the counter and edged through the crowd to take their order. She brought with her a bottle of Bollinger champagne.

"I didn't order this," Leonard said, his eyes popping at the sight of the label.

"Compliments of the owner," the young girl smiled, bending to fill their glasses. Leonard, feasting his eyes on the curve of her breasts, was immediately placated.

"The owner?" Sarah asked.

"Over there, by the bar." She pointed to a tall man standing alone and looking in their direction.

Sarah recognized the stranger. There could only be one broad-shouldered, tall, svelte bald man who could make her sweat and shiver in one same breath.

"Nicky! Did you tell him we were coming here?" Sarah was furious.

"Of course not. Don't you think if he owns this place he's entitled to be here?"

Sarah gave Nicky a scathing stare, then turned to glance at Julian.

"What?" Nicky asked, on the defensive. "Where Julian chooses to be is not my business, sweetie."

"Strange, don't you think? Mark cancels on me—mysteriously, I might add, and Julian appears—out of the blue."

He was looking directly at them, although she could not see his eyes. Strangely, he wore dark glasses. But he had not changed his position in the last three minutes. Of course, he was staring.

"Take it up with him, Sarah. Oh! I forgot. To do this, you'll have to talk to him." Nicky flashed her a toothy, mischievous smile.

Something was going on. Leonard did not even feign surprise.

Sarah saw Julian walking toward them. He was wearing a light-colored, perfectly tailored jacket over dark pants. Unable to look away, she swallowed nervously, distracted only by the flashing neon exit sign twenty feet away. Why did he always make her heart beat faster and her legs feel like putty?

The music was loud and thrashing a rhythmic beat. On cue or not, Julian was forcefully walking to that beat, looking dangerously sexy.

He stopped in front of their table, barely acknowledged Nicky and Leo, and extended his hand to her. She glimpsed the gold watch on his wrist, the huge hand and the long wide fingers that had driven her mad during their lovemaking. Though they looked like paws, his hands were surprisingly deft and delicate, like secret weapons, she fancied.

It was inevitable, she supposed. Nicky was right. She would have to face him in order to get some answers. She stood and smiled at him. She had made up her mind not to be intimidated by Julian, and taking his hand, followed him onto the dance floor—at least she hoped that's where he was taking her.

But against the back wall behind the counter, he opened a door and took her down a small corridor as Sarah fought not to panic; he opened another door and lead her through to a small room with its longest wall made out of glass. They could see the dancers mixing it up, the couples cuddling at the tables and the people coming in and out. They could also hear the music.

"Can they see us?" Sarah asked noticing that people were oblivious to them.

"It's a one-way mirror. Security sits here to stop trouble before it starts."

"Convenient for people who want to participate and not be seen," she told him, her voice a mocking scorn.

"I wouldn't know," he answered, finally removing his glasses. "I never come here. The smoke hurts my eyes," he indicated the glasses. "They're amber. They still allow me to see and they protect a little."

"How can you own a place where you never come?"

"A friend of mine needed the cash to buy it out, improve on it. She didn't want to owe me, so she gave me a full partnership."

A girl after her own heart, Sarah thought. She didn't want to owe Julian anything either.

He smiled at her and scooped her up in his arms. "You look nice tonight."

"Julian, what are you doing," she asked, unwilling to move out of his arms.

"You said we could be friends. I want to dance with you. May I?"

She was about to say that the rhythm was too fast to dance with their bodies entwined when he began moving to the beat of the music, taking wide steps, flexing over her, tipping her, twirling her to the beat only to land her body crashing against his, his hands rubbing the whole of her back.

Sarah was unfamiliar with the steps and for a few minutes, she concentrated on keeping up with him. This was probably the dirty dancing she had heard so much about. It was easy to do. His hands were directing her every move, anticipating, blocking and fondling all at once.

"What's this dance called?" she asked, winded and a little lightheaded.

He paused, his leg between hers, his eyes bolted to hers and gently, so as not to frighten her, he bent his head to kiss her but did not. Sarah made no move to avoid the kiss she felt sure was coming. But Julian simply stared at the anticipation on her face—her lips parted sensuously and her green eyes mere slits—and hung there, his lips touching hers without adding the slightest pressure. For a long minute, all that mingled in a passionate kiss was the warmth of their breath.

Sarah could no longer hear the music. All she could remember was once upon a time, his tongue had slid into her mouth, exploring, caressing and blissfully obstructing her breathing. All there was now was emptiness. She opened her mouth a little wider, and as she approached him to apply pressure to his lips, he moved back enough to moan her name.

"Don't you want to know why I am here?"

That's true. In her haste to follow him, in the gentle oblivion of his arms, she had forgotten all the questions she had for him.

She backed away, only now noticing that the stretchy sheath she was wearing had rolled up to her waist. It's no wonder he had had his legs between hers and was able to caress her thighs.

"Julian!" she protested as she quickly pulled down her dress and backed away from him. "What *are* you doing here?"

He smiled at her discountenance. "The old expression—if the mountain won't come to you, you find a way to go to the mountain. You still haven't answered my question."

"Is this what this is about?" She was stunned. "Wait a minute," she suddenly realized backing away even more. "You said you never come here. Why are you here—tonight, at the same time I am…? Who told you I would be here?"

"Now you're thinking, Miss Miller." He bowed his head with a mocking smile. "I am here specifically for you and only for you." This last phrase was soft and gentle. "Trust me," he added to her speechless, shocked facial expression, "you're the only one that could ever make me set foot in a place like this."

"Nicky told you I'd be here," she breathed. "She lied to me." This was more hurtful than anything else he had thrown her way.

"Nicky did not tell me you would be here. Relax. Your problem is that you jump to conclusions much too quickly."

"Then who…?"

Julian turned to look at the couples laughing it up and partying on the other side of the glass, and somehow wished he was out there with his girl, with Sarah. He turned back to face another kind of music. "Mark told me." He did not add anything else. There was no need. This time she needed to draw her own conclusions.

"Mark?" she breathed. "Why would Mark tell you where...did he ask you to come in his place...? He was short with me, abrupt almost. Julian," it suddenly dawned on her. "What did Mark and you discuss? You didn't...." She could not, would not phrase it. If she didn't put her doubts into words, it would be fine. He was right. She jumped to conclusions much too fast. But the look on his face, that I-did-it-for-your-own-good-you'll-thank-me-later look, framed its own answer.

She felt faint, scared and plainly overwhelmed by the intent in his eyes. She backed up so that she could lean against the wall—be closer to the door. It might help her breathe, she thought. "You didn't...you had promised me that he wouldn't hear it from you..."

"I had to."

All the while Sarah just kept shaking her head. It wasn't happening, she thought. It was all a bad dream—this room, her naked feelings. She was going to wake up all sweaty in her bed and be terribly glad it had just been a silly dream; that's what it was.

"He laughed at me when I told him I'd been in love with you for the past two years. Then he got serious on me and told me you loved him. That you had said as much...Imagine my fury, me still looking for a simple answer from you. I guess that's when he must have seen how determined I was—the anger in my eyes. He blurted out that the two of you would go away, if it made it easier for me."

"You didn't...I can't believe..."

"Sarah..."

When Julian stepped toward her, she turned the door handle. Escaping was uppermost on her mind. She had to flee. Then she realized the handle was jammed and not turning. "You locked the door?" She was furious.

"We're going to have this out," he spoke forcefully. "I'm not leaving and neither are you, not before we are clear on a lot more than this." He grabbed her wrists and tried to steady her. "Stop it. There's nowhere to run. No one can hear you. The room is sound proof; and no one can see you."

"Oh, my god!" she breathed. "You are a maniac!" she flung at him. All she wanted to do was hurt him and she didn't care how she did it.

"Mark was hurt, Sarah. He read my face. He saw the love I feel for you. I couldn't hide it. He tried to punch me, and when he couldn't fight me physically, he lashed out at me the best way he knew how." Julian let her go. He bent from the waist, his hands on his knees. "You don't understand," he muttered. "This was my baby brother I'd spent a lifetime protecting. Against a drunken, raging lunatic for a father. Against an over-protective, over-dependent mother. Against school bullies." He redressed to look into her angry eyes. "Part of me wanted to shelter him from the truth. Part of me urged I come clean." He took in a long shaky breath as he turned his back to her. "It was the hardest thing I ever had to do, Sarah.

And I was walking away. I wasn't going to tell him. As much as I love you, as much as I need you, I was going to step back and let the two of you decide my fate." Julian turned to look at her again.

Sarah thought she saw tears in his eyes.

"Then he boasted. In a fit of rage, he declared that you would never be mine. That you could never make love to a simian like me…'It's already done'—was all I said. He calmed down once I'd admitted this. Somewhere, deep down, I think he knew."

"Then what happened?" Sarah's voice was small and breathless.

Julian shrugged, staring at his shoes. "A few minutes passed—an eternity. He just had one question."

Sarah looked at him anxiously waiting for him to continue.

"He asked me when. I told him. He nodded, apologized about the scuffle and left. The next day I found a note from him at the mid-town gym. He'd scribbled a few words, slipped the paper in an envelope and left it with Mickey. It just read that you'd be here on Friday night for the last party."

Sarah's legs were weak. Since there was no point in fighting to get out, she walked over to a sofa in the corner and sat down, her mind juggling with what she had heard. Of course, she realized Julian had briefly summed up what must have been a huge and long altercation between him and Mark. She had come between two brothers. The pain Julian had felt faced with that onus still glared in his drawn mouth and sullen eyes.

"Whatever possessed you to take this matter into your own hands, Julian? Why not discuss this with me first?"

"Because I was told—in no uncertain terms—that you are in love with me, all you do is talk about me incessantly, that Mark is not the man for you and that you were devastated about the possibility of creating a rift between two brothers."

Sarah drew in a squeaky breath, putting her hand in front of her mouth. "That was told in confidence to Nicky. How dare you force her to tell you my personal feelings?"

He raised his eyebrows and his admonishing eyes told their tale.

"I can't believe she would tell you this. What else did she tell you?"

"She came to see me at the gym, in Brooklyn…"

"No!"

"Don't be mad at her. She loves you, Sarah. She's very worried about you. Insisted you had your tail caught in a catch-22 dilemma. She didn't go into details…although the word ravish did come into play." He gave her a knowing look.

Sarah blushed, her eyes immediately darting to the dancers on the other side of the wall as if her eyes could attach themselves to Nicky and nail her where she sat. "One can't trust anyone with a secret these days. Do you really intend keeping me here against my will?"

"Keeping you, yes. But is it against your will?" He scrutinized her carefully.

Again Sarah colored. "I can't think straight, Julian. Not after all I've just learned. Trust me, the answer you're seeking is not in me right now. I would rather we meet tomorrow, in a more civilized area."

"Ah, yes! The not-thinking-straight routine—a faculty you apparently lack in my presence—as also told to me." He smiled, irritated by her discomfort. "Won't the same decision be just as difficult to render another day—another time… while in my presence?"

Sarah was irate. She rose and stormed toward the door. "You can't keep me imprisoned here," she defied him, glaring at him, her chest heaving laboriously.

For a long excruciating minute Julian glared back at her, the same dark expression he had worn on that cursed Saturday evening. Somewhere in the back of his mind, he remembered Nicky's words about not bullying Sarah. If there was ever a place and time where he could redeem Sara's trust and esteem for him, it was here and now. Letting her go when they both knew he had complete hold over her—physically and emotionally—should prove to her he was truly in love.

"Where would you like to meet tomorrow?" he asked her roughly.

"Can I call you in the morning and arrange it?" she whispered.

He smiled, knowing fully that she was paying him lip

service. She had no intention of meeting with him tomorrow. He bent and kissed her lips. "I'll be waiting impatiently, Sarah."

Julian reached inside his jacket, removing the keys from an inside pocket, and toyed with his cell phone clipped to his belt.

"Expecting a phone call?" Sarah murmured.

Julian looked at her squarely as he automatically punched a couple of keys on the phone's pad. "I wish that's what this was," he answered enigmatically. He replaced the phone on the clip on his belt and turned to unlock the door. Sarah had to steel herself not to bolt.

"Off the topic," Julian told her as he held a firm grip on her hand. "Your friend Daniel is going to be alright."

"I know. I saw him at the Center. He needs to recuperate, but he'll be fine."

"No. I mean, he won't have to move or something just as drastic. He no longer has a hit hanging over his head."

"They've arrested the guy who did this?"

Julian smiled. "They would never been able to make it stick."

"Then how…"

"Turns out, a little birdie told me recently, if you want to put a contract out on someone in New York City, there's a particular pecking order that needs to be respected. When it isn't, the hunter becomes the hunted, and Nature once more finds its proper balance."

"Sounds like you have friends in low places."

"High places, low places...Somehow, they all meet up somewhere in the middle."

Sarah smiled at him and told him she was going to the ladies' room.

Julian nodded and watched her leave, sadness in his eyes. He knew she was bolting for the door. She was too angry with cousin and her beau to lag behind.

When Sarah reached the cool night air, she remembered she had checked her coat. Luckily she had her bag with her. That's all she really needed, she told herself, hugging her arms to stop the shivering. She searched the club's grounds for a taxi, but at this hour the stand was empty. It would be difficult to find one. The thought struck her that she might not have enough cash. She inventoried her purse and found a lame ten dollar bill. That would not cover the fare to her apartment.

"Miss Sarah!"

Sarah turned to the sound of a familiar voice calling her name repeatedly. A taxi driver was standing by the curve with the passenger door to his car wide open, his bright smile inviting her to step inside the vehicle.

She walked toward it, stunned to see him there. "Jeff, isn't it?"

He nodded expansively.

She hesitated by the door. "What a coincidence meeting you here like this," Sarah uttered quizzically without quite believing.

"No coincidence," he answered politely with a friendly grin. "Mr. Julian called me."

So that was the meaning of Julian's cryptic response about preferring an incoming call.

"His cell phone reaches my pager. I always come for Mr. Julian. I just called him from outside. He told me to look for you."

Sarah shook her head, bewildered by Julian's formidable means. She had thought she was so clever, running away. He knew she was leaving, and he had not only allowed her to walk out, he had called the cab to take her home.

She hesitated by the curb, angry she wasn't going to get to stomp away. But it wasn't Jeff's fault. To ignore his kind gesture to take her home would hurt this innocent man's feelings. Sarah sighed and hopped in, allowing Jeff to close the door behind her.

When time came for her to settle the fare, he refused to discuss it. "Mr. Julian pays me handsomely," he insisted.

CHAPTER ELEVEN

For the next few days, Sarah refused to see anyone. Of course, she did not call Julian. In essence, calling him tomorrow, as a broad general term, could mean she would call him anytime in the near or distant future, she consoled herself whenever the nagging thought of not being true to her word threatened to put her to shame. She had not even taken Nicky's persistent calls or acknowledged the impromptu visit she had paid her the following Wednesday.

Jorge had buzzed her, stating a cousin of hers was in the foyer asking to go up. Sarah had refused to see her. She was indisposed and feeling ill. She had left her intercom open and listened to the altercation between the two. Nicky had threatened Jorge, calling him incompetent and inefficient, while Jorge had threatened to call the police. He had stated with much affectation that Miss Miller did not wish to be disturbed and that he was there to uphold her wishes.

Dear Jorge, Sarah had thought, it's no wonder people in the building referred to him as Boy Jorge behind his back. She was grateful for his intervention. She just could not face Nicky. She could not chance an argument that could echo between them for years, endangering their friendship. She needed to clear her head, to calm down and let the fumes evaporate before she talked to anyone about how she felt. Nicky needed to explain her side of things, she realized. But forgiveness was beyond her strained nerves at this point. Mark had not called either—as he had promised he would, and she of all people understood how he was also dodging the dreaded frank discussion.

As for Julian, she tucked him conveniently away in a corner of her mind, concentrating instead on her music, applying herself to her craft with renewed effort, honing her skills in preparation for the string of concerts scheduled over the next three months. She had crossed Frank and Bella's path once or twice. Bella was the same with her—all smiles, very solicitous. Frank seemed different, shy and awkward in her presence. And while she had wondered if he knew about her and Julian that day after the party, she now concluded that Frank had two sources of information, Julian and Mark, doubling the probability that he knew of their precarious triangle.

Sarah had just ended a full day of practice at the Rose

Rehearsal Studio. She had chalked it up to practice, but it had served as a performance for the Alumni Chapter of Julliard. They were holding meetings and reunions over the next two weeks, and the Rose Studio was one of their first ports of call. Daniel had brought a recording of his music and received rave reviews. His arm was healing fast and he and Sarah had demonstrated their skill at harmonious accords through a piece they had played on the piano, Sarah with her right hand, Daniel with his left. Sarah lacked the practice, but the piano had been the first instrument she had learned to play as a child.

Photographers had swarmed to the antechamber later that afternoon, so by six o'clock Sarah and her friends were tired and duly famished.

On her way out of the Center with a group of her fellow musicians, just outside the foyer, she bumped into Nicky who had been sitting in the lobby waiting for her.

"Hey, is this a bad time to get together?" Nicky asked humbly.

Sarah stopped to look at her and told her friends to go on without her. There was audible disappointment, so she told them she had a previous engagement she had forgotten about. Turning toward Nicky, she smiled. "It's good to see you, Nicky. I've been meaning to call you…I've just been too embarrassed to do so."

Nicky ran up to her and hugged her as hard as she could. "You big ninny. I'm the idiot. Why should you be embarrassed?" Nicky quickly dabbed at a few tears. "It's been a month. Were you ever going to call?"

Sarah stroked her hair. "The very next call I made," she told her with a teary smile.

"Let's get out of here. I'll treat you to dinner."

"What about Leonard? Isn't Thursday you're special evening?"

Nicky looked at her, a wry expression on her face. "We broke up. It's nothing." She forestalled Sarah's concerned apology. "I'll tell you about it later."

Nicky surveyed Sarah's appearance. She was wearing flared hip-hugging black satin pants, a pale green blouse and a sleeveless vest. "Hum! You'll do. I'm treating. We're eating at Aix tonight." She smiled. "That's why I'm wearing a skirt." Nicky refused to hop a bus. She hailed a cab and despite the Upper West Side's traffic, they walked in the door of the restaurant less than twenty minutes later.

The restaurant was one Sarah and Nicky had promised themselves they'd try. It was new and offered the crispy squab Sarah was dying to sample.

Sitting at a booth by the window, Sarah just had to ask. "So how are you affording all this, exactly? Are you using your monthly student wages to pay for this one meal?"

"I figure you're worth it," she winked. "I'm not a total moron. I have some savings. Besides, I figure that once your inheritance comes in, all my financial woes will be a distant memory."

Sarah smiled and patted her hand. "You can say that again. It'll be great. You can pay off all your student loans, your accumulated debts, start your own practice…"

"Whoa there, sweetie! I was just joking. But if you insist…" Nicky gave Sarah a teasing smile. "Any news from France?"

"I've signed papers releasing the vineyards. Oh! And I have a flight booked in a month from now to meet with the notary."

The girls interrupted their conversation while the waiter brought more bread, oven treats and white Chablis.

"Oh! And I spoke to Simon, the younger of my grandfather's stepbrothers. He's very nice. He invited me to stay with them when I go to France."

"Does he know about the attempt…?" Nicky cleared her throat and waylaid her question as the waiter circled their table with fresh water and left with their order.

"Yes. And Serge is not his son, by the way. He was a hired hand who worked for them a few years back. He was approached by two of the lawyers who control the finances for the vineyards and paid an enormous sum of money to try to sway me to sign over the vineyards to the law firm. Serge thought he could have it all by having me agree to marry him."

"The attempt on your life…who's responsible?"

"Serge maintains he didn't know there was any such plan. I guess the lawyers became frustrated when Serge and I broke off our engagement."

"So, your…uncles or great-uncles never had anything to do with this?"

Sarah shook her head. "They had already proposed in a letter to my lawyer that the entente between my grandfather and themselves be continued under the new will's stipulations. The letter was intercepted by their lawyers, who would have loved to purchase it for the proverbial dollar or for some token value and then sell it back to them at a huge profit."

"I can understand why. One hundred and fifty million dollars is nice personal freedom," Nicky said dreamily.

"I meant it—about you sharing in the wealth, Nicky."

"I know you did, sweetie. We'll just have to take it slowly. I'm far from ready to open my own practice. I still have a lot to study about human nature before I dare step out on that limb again with homemade advice. The experience with Julian left me smarting. I thought I was helping you both and…well, who knew he had such loose lips. I mean, first he meddles between you and Mark…"

"How do you know this?" Sarah waited for the waiter to deposit their entrees and leave. "Julian only told me that night, in a secluded area." Sarah was surprised.

"He came to see us at the table afterwards. He reminded me to grab your coat before leaving—which I have, by the way, so don't worry."

"You mean he told you what we'd discussed?"

"Well, I don't know that he did. He told Leonard and

me that he'd spoken to Mark—told him how he felt. He gave Leonard a few details of their argument—wanted his advice. That's when Leo asked him what fool had suggested he do this in the first place."

"Don't tell me, that's when the squabble ensued between you and Leo?"

"Pretty much. It began at the club and ended two weeks later, when I kicked him out of my life."

"I'm so sorry, Nicky. I wish I'd known. When I asked Julian why he'd taken it upon himself to talk to Mark, he said you'd gone to see him and...well, you'd told him I was in love with him..."

"Man! Sarah, I thought that's what might have happened—why you were so angry with me. Who knew the jerk would discuss everything I'd told him in strictest confidence—to help him, no less. I tell you, Sarah. Never saw that curve rounding the corner." Nicky took a sip of her white wine. "How did you get home, anyway? Leonard and I had to walk three blocks just to get a cab. I was so worried about you."

Sarah shook her head from side to side, still stunned by it. "Julian had paged Jeff—the family's designated cabby—and he was waiting for me outside the door."

Nicky's surprise forced her to swallow a small piece of trout the wrong way, and she coughed it up with rounded, red eyes. "You're kidding," she finally uttered with a cracked voice. "I can't believe he knew you'd stomp out. Does he have a crystal ball, or what?"

"The man is just extremely tuned to me somehow. I've had lots of time to think about him and me this past month—not that I haven't tried to forget about him—more often than not. Sometimes I think Julian sees clear through me—knows me better than I know myself. That's probably what originally scared me about him."

"You're not scared of him anymore?"

Sarah shook her head, a slight smile tugging at the corner of her mouth. "Now I have to find a way to talk to Mark. So much time has gone by…"

"You mean he never called you—when he said he would?"

Sarah shrugged. "I can't say I blame him. I did the same thing to Julian. I assured him I'd call the next day to arrange a meeting between us, and I never did. I guess that's one more thing Mark and I have in common. We're both cowards."

"Don't beat yourself up. You've been through a lot, maybe half of which is Julian's fault."

"I'm way past caring whose fault lies behind the mess. It doesn't matter. I've pretty much decided what needs to be done."

"You have?" Nicky was ecstatic. To finally know Sarah's decision…"Oh, my god! What are the odds?" Nicky squeezed Sarah's hands. "Don't look now, but someone you know just walked in behind you—with a lady on his arm."

If she had not been sitting, Sarah's heart would have

plummeted to her feet. The thought of Julian having replaced her with someone else was physically painful. "Not…"

"Yes!" exclaimed Nicky, unknowingly torturing Sarah beyond breaking point. "Mr. Personality himself, the man of the hour, strutting tall with a blond beauty on his Armani-clad arm. Okay, you can look now. He's facing the waiter."

Sarah turned, caught sight of Mark's head and shoulders and breathed such a sigh of relief that Nicky perceived it as deep disappointment.

"Don't let it bother you too much, Sarah. I never thought the man was your type."

"I'm not surprised, Nicky. Nor am I disappointed. You can't expect him to live like a monk—especially after what Julian told him."

"At least now you know why he was in no hurry to call you. Looks like he mends fences quickly. Are you still going to have the talk?"

Sarah nodded. "I need to clear the air. This will just make it easier."

"Lucked out again," Nicky mumbled, seconds before lowering her eyes. "The seating hostess is bringing them this way."

Sarah braced herself for the encounter, still hoping they would walk by and not notice them. But smooth and wrinkle free this dinner was not going to be.

As Mark came toward their table, Sarah had her back to him, and since he was only paying attention to the girl on his arm, he did not see the two women at the table on his left. But when the hostess stopped at the table next to theirs, the reunion was inevitable. As soon as Mark sat down, he was facing Sarah.

He stared at her and took a few seconds to register who she was. Sarah saw the recognition on his face when he paled, looking extremely nervous. At first, he appeared bent on pretending she was not there, leaning toward ignoring her completely. But at second glance, he smiled and greeted them both.

"It's nice to see you, Sarah," he said softly, "Nicky also. I would like you to meet Jessica Raines. She's the arts critic for Symphony Magazine."

"I'm pleased to meet you," Sarah smiled politely. "I'm Sarah Miller, and this is my cousin, Nicole Miller. I've read your column; some of your opinions are fresh and very interesting."

"Thank you. It's an honor to meet the newest member of the Quartet." Jessica smiled, "And the darling who stole our Julian's heart."

Sarah was stunned that Jessica would know this, even more shocked since she detected a dose of cattiness in her last remark. Had this beautiful woman decided to claw her fangs into Julian rather than into Mark?

"Julian's heart is very much his own, Miss Raines," Sarah answered in the same tone.

"Not...the last time I checked—and, Miss Miller, being

a reporter, I am very observant."

That clinched it, concluded Sarah. This woman's claws were six inches long. Her smile spoke of rejection, envy, and was not devoid of the breath of a threat. Julian was definitely on her menu and Sarah suddenly felt a pang of remorse for the way she was treating Mark. For the way he was being publicly discarded by this femme fatale.

The waiter came to Mark's table, distracting their conversation, and Sarah indicated to Nicky with willful eyes that she wanted to leave.

"But you haven't even touched your food," whispered Nicky. But one more look at Sarah's imploring eyes changed her mind. "May we have the check please?" Nicky asked the waiter, once he had finished taking Mark and Jessica's order.

"Certainly," he answered and hurried away.

"You're not leaving already?" Mark asked, his eyes traveling kindly over Sarah's face, taking in the fact that their dinner plates were still full.

"I have an early day tomorrow," Sarah answered him. "Mark…" She hesitated, but when she saw how eagerly he waited, she continued, "May I call you tomorrow? I have tickets to a play on Saturday that you might like to attend."

"Yes, do so," he smiled broadly. "I would enjoy that very much."

Sarah noticed his response was warm and he appeared extremely interested—perhaps partly to stick it to his partner of the moment. Sarah was only too pleased to hand him back a bit of his dignity.

"It's a date then," she smiled. "Talk to you soon."

Nicky and she left without another word. Once outside, Nicky bent over with hysterical laughter. "I can't believe you did that. Oh, geez, crap! You've just infuriated the arts critic for Symphony Magazine. Did you see the murderous look on her face? I thought she was going to jump up and scratch your eyes out." Nicky stopped laughing, coming up for air.

"I still can't believe she knows about Julian and me. Does the whole city know about us? She is a reporter!" Sarah was not laughing.

"Sarah, do you realize what you've done? Who you've alienated?"

Sarah stretched her arm to hail a cab. "Looks like the deed was done when she walked in there. She hated me at a glance. You heard her; she openly accused me of stealing her precious Julian's heart."

"Your precious Julian's heart," Nicky smiled at her.

Sarah nodded, a knowing smile on her face. "Who ever said publicity comes cheap…"

They settled into the cab and Nicky had to ask, remembering how close she had come to hearing Sarah's heart-to-heart, "Are you really going to date Mark again?"

Sarah thought she had detected a faint catch in Nicky's voice.

"Don't worry. I'm not about to lead him on or anything. I intend squaring things with him immediately, proposing friendship, explaining my feelings more clearly. It's taken me this long to sort through my own heart. I'm not about to start playing with someone else's."

Nicky squeezed her hand, not daring to prod any deeper. She knew Sarah's feelings were still too tentative to stand scrutiny.

"What about you, Nicky? Any chance of reconciliation between you and Leo—or should I say, any desire to do so?"

"None, none whatsoever. I'm hunting fresh game. I want someone who will really love me. Someone who won't need exterior stimuli to be in the mood," she raised her eyebrows. "Know what I mean?"

Sarah nodded, staring out the car window. She had known someone like that once. Was he still interested, available? She might have needed time off from Julian to rein in her scattered spirits, but she could not help wondering why he had not bothered to show her any signs of life. He could not be angry with her for the way she had left; he was the one who had provided the transportation. Had he buried his love for her so deeply he could no longer resurrect it? Did the Jessica Raines of this world exert pressures too delicious, too tempting to ward off?

There were many such questions that haunted Sarah's nights, her sleep, her waking hours. And as the shadows grew, so did the fear of facing these questions. Until picking up a phone to hear the voice she craved to hear was equivalent to lifting a hundred-pound weight. Yet she had convinced herself that she needed the prolonged estrangement. Though the passage of time made the subject harder to broach, the distance provided a clearer, less daunting picture.

But running into Mark at the restaurant had brought it all back full force—Julian and the intimidation she felt around him, Renny's protection, the fear for her life, the outings with Mark and the children. Until then, she had not realized how much she had missed it. So she was glad when Mark showed up on her doorstep, punctual as usual. She had been counting the hours until their visit.

When she opened her door, she couldn't help thinking how handsome he was, dressed in a casual pale-colored jacket.

"You ready?" He smiled, taking her hand.

Sarah nodded. Jeff was waiting in the cab downstairs to whisk them off to the Manhattan Theatre Club.

"It's a new production by Daniel Stern," Sarah told him, settling into the back of the car. "I think you'll like it. It's a comedy, with John Pankow and Julie White." Sarah punctuated the strained silence with as much filler as she could.

Mark turned toward her, smiling comfortably as he glanced at the hair she'd left loose—as he liked it—her shimmering top, the long easy flowing skirt she had donned and the care she had given her light make-up. "Sarah, let's not allow the past to create even one awkward minute between us." He waited for some sign from her to continue.

She nodded. "I agree."

"I can't pretend I totally understand what happened between you and…" He glanced toward the front seat, toward Jeff, and lowered his voice. "Well you know who I mean."

Sarah was glad he had broached the subject early. They could both breathe easier now. "I'm sorry I didn't tell you sooner. You think you don't understand—hey! It was happening to me, Mark, and I didn't understand it at all."

He smiled, just happy to be with her. He took her hands in his and fastened his eyes tightly to hers.

Sarah knew she would have to straighten out their relationship as soon as possible.

She pulled her hands away. "Mark," she hesitated biting her lower lip. "You and I are so similar—I guess that's why I was so drawn to you from the beginning. We enjoy the same composers, we're both musicians, we laugh at the same things…I guess I mistook this camaraderie, this pleasure to be with you for…I won't say for love because in a way, I do love you…"

"I hear you. I feel the exact same way. I get goofy inside just knowing I'm going to spend an evening with you. But when it's time to kiss you and take it further…well, let's just say I never minded you withdrawing from my steamier advances. The pleasure stops at staring into your eyes and holding your hand. I can't explain it. When…he told me what had happened between the two of you, I was angry—livid is probably a better word…"

"I'm so sorry, Mark…"

"No, not angry with you. Not even angry with…Angry with myself for not realizing it sooner. To need to have it pointed out to me…Anyway, my lashing out at Julian was just hurt pride—you know, big brother encroaching on my territory—how dare he and all that."

"How is Julian?" Sarah all of a sudden could not refrain from asking.

Mark's smile grew wider and he flashed her a hint of teasing. "Coward," he admonished. "Why not find out for yourself. You know you're dying to talk to him."

"Well, I don't know that he feels the same way—anymore." She threw Mark a sidelong glance.

"Oh! No you don't, Sarah Miller," he laughed. "Anything you want to know about Julian, you're going to have to ask him yourself." He paused to look out the window, trying to find his bearings. "We're almost there. Do you have a program I can browse?"

She nodded and took out of her purse a little booklet she had tucked away. They thanked Jeff and Mark paid him for the fare. Sarah handed Mark the program. They joined the growing line of waiting fans while he familiarized himself with the story.

Once comfortably seated, Mark glanced at Sarah in the dimness of the theater and looped an arm around her shoulders. He bent close to her ear. "He's miserable, you know—Julian."

Sarah turned and looked at him. Even in the half-light,

she spotted a mischievous glint dancing in his eyes.

"It serves him right," he answered, anticipating her question. But then Mark became serious all at once. "I've never seen him like this—not even when our father left and he was facing insurmountable odds."

Sarah's heart sank. She closed her eyes, trying not to see Julian's eyes boring into hers, and concentrated on losing herself in the moment. She was going to enjoy this play.

As it turned out, they both did. The plot was funny, the dialogue witty and the evening passed quickly, as if in a flash.

Outside, in the balmy breezy night air, on the sidewalk congested with people, Mark tugged at Sarah's arm and ran with her to the nearest café, while there were still small tables left unoccupied. He ordered them both amaretto cappuccinos. "Would you like anything else with that, Sarah?"

"No. Thank you. I laughed so hard. Wasn't that just hilarious?"

"It was, sweetie." Mark looked at her with wistful eyes and after the slightest of hesitations, bent to kiss her lips gently.

Sarah returned the friendly peck on the lips and felt a bout of shyness creep up unexpectedly. "You must be wondering..."

"No, no," Mark forestalled her. "You don't have to defend what you and Julian did that night, what craziness swept over you. I've given this a lot of thought, Sarah. I've already moved on. Unlike my brother, I rarely get attached to one woman for very long." He smiled. "Please, let's just leave it at that—can you do that for me?"

Sarah nodded, moving closer to give him a hug.

"One more thing. Is your cousin Nicky seeing anyone?"

Sarah's eyes widened. "You want to date my cousin Nicky?"

"Do you think she'd like that?"

Sarah knew she would, especially as she had caught a little glimpse of admiration in Nicky's eyes whenever she looked at Mark. "I must warn you, unattachable man, my cousin needs permanency in her life right now. She's looking for a keeper."

"What a fine coincidence," he smiled, mocking her tone of voice.

"But you just said…"

"Fast is in the past. Nowadays, I'm more inclined to look for something to last."

"So, what are you waiting for—my blessing?"

"I wanted to make sure you wouldn't be offended if I did this. Frankly, you still haven't approached Julian; and here we are you and I…"

"Who ever said that my heart—my life, had to belong to either one of you Spinner men?" Sarah laughed at the shocked expression on his face. "You had better hurry and ask Nicky out before I spill the beans. Seems common in your family for people to air out their secrets."

"What does that mean?"

"Well, Julian had no qualms telling you about him and me. I'm quasi-certain he blabbed to Frank 'cause the man looks at me strangely ever since that...night. And..."

"Listen, Sarah. I'm the last one who would want to defend Julian's behavior. But if you remember the afternoon of the party..."

"I don't think I'll ever forget it," she smiled.

"...had circumstances been a tad different, you and I might have landed in bed together."

Sarah had to admit that this was true.

"I can't morally blame Julian for getting there first, can I?" He stroked Sarah's hot cheeks. "As for Frank knowing... Julian came downstairs early that morning. Frank apparently found him in the kitchen pacing furiously and muttering to himself. He was so bewildered and down on himself that it took weak-hearted Frank an hour to calm him down. I guess dregs of what had happened finally surfaced—at least enough for Frank to piece it together."

"I suspected he knew."

"He's the one who suggested Julian leave and not be there when you came down. They argued that point. Julian wanted to stay, face you and beg your forgiveness. My big brother is nothing if not thorough, and absolutely accountable for everything he does."

"How do you know this?"

"Julian told me, that night we fought. I asked him who else knew."

"What about that reporter, Rebecca Raines? Why would she say…"

Mark laughed as Sarah's earlier comment of spilled secrets came to roost. "I guess you're right, Sarah. There aren't many secrets we can keep."

"By we, I take it you mean Julian?"

He nodded. "He can be stoic and strong. He never complains about anyone, or discusses other people's business. He is a private person. But he is also hot-blooded and fiery. When something happens to him or to someone he loves, he's quick to react. He'll claim responsibility for any of his errors, intentional or otherwise. That's his nature. Jessica Raines has been trying to rope him for the last three weeks. He told her he could never love anyone else but you. He just likes to call things by their name."

"Why by my name? I still can't believe he said that, you know," Sarah snorted, shaking her head while she finished the last dregs of her cappuccino.

"He loves you Sarah…"

"He has a funny way of showing it, Mark. She's a reporter for heaven's sake. Doesn't he know that this is liable to get around and…"

"…And what? It's just Julian's crazy way of displaying his loyalty."

"Or of tying me to a *fait accompli*." Knowing Julian,

Sarah knew that this particular reason was not beyond his means.

Mark smiled broadly. "Clever, my brother. Personally, I wouldn't have thought of it. But you're right. What better way to claim you than to announce to the world that the two of you are a couple."

CHAPTER TWELVE

It was this disturbing, nagging thought that had Sarah flexing her fingers by the phone the next evening, angry one minute, calm the next. Whenever she imagined Julian manipulating and controlling her, she would walk away, cursing the sordid telephone. When she focused on all that he had done for her, selflessly, she would stroke the receiver in an effort to gain the strength to pick it up.

"Hello, I'd like to speak to Mr. Spinner—Julian Spinner," Sarah asked a feminine voice she assumed was the baby sitter. The nanny would have left by now.

"I'm afraid he's busy at the moment. May I tell him whose calling?"

"Yes, please tell him it's Sarah."

"Oh! Right," the woman exclaimed enthusiastically. "I'll tell him straight away."

Sarah waited patiently, her eyes closed, rehearsing what she planned to tell him.

Sarah was surprised when the baby sitter came back to the phone.

"I'm sorry, miss. He says he is busy for the next ten minutes or so. Then he has a dinner engagement. He asks if you can call him tomorrow."

Sarah hesitated for a couple of seconds. "Did you tell him who it was?"

"Yes, I did. I'm sorry it's such a bad time."

"Thank you." Sarah hung up the phone, pale and upset. She sat down in the lounger next to the table and wondered if Julian wasn't deliberately giving her the brush-off. Maybe he had decided he had waited long enough. He had written her off completely. Maybe he had given in to Miss Raines after all, unless his dinner date was with someone else. She shook her head, thinking that it did not make sense. Mark had just finished telling her how upset Julian was. Even Jessica Raines had asserted that Julian's heart belonged to Sarah. There could not have been that drastic a change since Thursday night.

Then Sarah remembered how fast her own life had turned—on a dime, one might say—the day of Brad's birthday party. Suppose Jessica Raines had told Julian about the date she had made with Mark for Saturday evening. Was theatre with Mark the proverbial drop that had tipped the bucket—for a proud man like Julian? Jessica was the type to use this sort of stratagem to capture Julian's fancy. Sarah was sure of it.

She suddenly had the urge to call back and ask for Mark's help. But what could Mark do? Julian wouldn't listen to him—not where she was concerned.

She began pacing up and down her small living room, her eyes riveted to the telephone, and she jumped when she heard it ring; once, twice…

"Hello?"

"You'll never guess who I'm going out with this evening—not in a thousand years."

"Hi, Nicky." Sarah let out a tremulous sigh but smiled nevertheless, faced with her cousin's obvious delight.

"What's the matter? You sound disappointed. Were you expecting someone else?"

That Nicky! She sure was a mind reader, Sarah thought, unwilling to confide just yet. "No, the phone startled me. So who's this hot date you have?" Sarah asked, not wanting to spoil her pleasure.

"Mark Spinner called me this afternoon. He invited me to dinner."

There was a small squeak of glee in the background; Sarah guessed it had to be Nicky jumping around at the other end of the phone. "Nicky! That's wonderful—I think. Is it?"

"Are you kidding? It's fantasmic, stupendful." Made-up words that sprang out of an overflowing heart. Nicky was laughing. "I was such a slut, Sarah. I said yes without even taking five seconds to think about it. Do you think I should have made him linger a bit first?" she asked, all at once seriously concerned.

"You did the right thing, Nicky. There's nothing worse than starting off a relationship by playing games. Make sure you're clear on all of your feelings with him."

"I want your blessing, Sarah. I know you say Mark and you are just friends, and I know you love Julian and all…but is this okay? If it's not…"

"Mark and I are all squared away. I told you, we could be brother and sister, as close as we are without having sex."

"How 'bout settling for brother and sister—in-law…" Nicky laughed. "You call Julian or…or I'll meddle again; I mean it."

Sarah promised she would and pre-ordered date details from Nicky.

The phone call over, Sarah sat on the couch by the window. Nicky had known all along that Mark was the man of her dreams—not consciously, but somewhere in the heart region. This also explained her adamancy about Mark and Sarah not meshing well. She had been right about her and Julian, too. She should have listened to her sooner. Now Julian seemed determined to move on. She had taken too long to decode her own heart.

A loud banging on the door woke Sarah. She had fallen asleep on the sofa, because it was dark now—past 9:00, she noticed on her watch—and she had the sore neck to prove it. It was not a dream. The loud thudding on her door continued.

"Okay, okay! There's no need to bang the door down. I'm coming," Sarah yelled out. She peeped through the small hole into the hallway but couldn't see anyone. Keeping the chain on the lock, she unfastened the deadbolts and opened just a crack, asking the caller to identify himself.

"Let me in, you two-bit hussy."

Sarah sighed. This comment alone from anyone other than Renny would have sent her calling security. Where was Jorge anyway, she wondered.

She opened the door, allowing entry to a fuming Renny, wondering ruefully what she had done now. Sarah moved aside and patiently resigned herself to the burst of a storm cloud.

"I trusted you, you two-timin' bitch!" Renny was walking up to her, dangerously close. Sarah had to back up against the wall.

"Renny, calm down. You're not going to get anywhere by swearing at me." Sarah was concerned but determined not to let it show.

"Look, I told you not to break Julie's heart. I told you to give him some. I told you how he felt. Nah! Miss Goody-two-shoes had to play him like she plays her fiddle—strong and mean." Hands on hips, hair swept back, Renny was dressed in black, emulating the perfect she-creature, sleek, feral and ferocious.

"Why don't you start by telling me what this is all

about?" Sarah's voice was calm and controlled. She advanced toward Renny, unafraid, looking her straight in the eye.

"Julie's in shreds. He hurts on account o' you're such a frigid bitch. He told me about you and Mark. How you asked Mark out—after all this time—to the theatre…and how Mark never came home Saturday night."

"What are you talking about? Yes, Mark and I went to the theatre. I asked him out, yes. I wanted to clear the air—tell him I thought we were mostly good friends. That there was nothing romantic between us. Mark agreed with me—not that it's any of your business."

Renny stood down and backed off a couple of steps. "Then where did Mark spend the night?"

"How should I know? The play finished at 9:30. We grabbed a couple of cappuccinos at the café across the alley, then Jeff drove me home."

"Jeff drove you?"

"Yes. As far as I know, he drove Mark home afterwards. We said our goodbyes in the cab."

"Since when does Mark call on Jeff?" Renny asked, her eyes squinting at Sarah.

"How should I know?" Sarah flung.

"Where was his car?"

"He said it was in the shop. He had left it and was picking it up sometime this morning…I think…" Sarah trailed off, just now realizing the huge misunderstanding her outing with Mark had caused. "So that's why he refused to take my call," she spoke more to herself.

"Who wouldn't take your call?"

"Julian." Sarah added pensively, "He gave the sitter some lame excuse about a dinner engagement...didn't even bother to tell me himself."

"That's a lie. Julie would never do that." Once again Renny was waving an accusing finger at her. "You could skin him alive and he'd still take your call. There ain't nothin' you can do to him that he wouldn't turn around and love you."

Sarah was on the verge of tears.

"That's how crazy he is about you. The man's nuts. He thinks you spent the night with his brother and I gotta tie him down so he won't come over here and make a fool of himself—beggin' you to love him instead."

Renny's words made Sarah dizzy. She grabbed the back of a chair. *If only it were true...*"Renny, I swear to you. I called Julian, gave the sitter my name..."

"Was it Aggie?"

Sarah shrugged. "I don't know. I assumed it was the sitter because it was 7:30 and I know the nanny was gone."

Renny thought for a while. "Julie doesn't know you called. I know it. He would've told me."

"Listen, Renny, Julian is very upset with me right now—and for no reason. I never loved his brother. Actually, Mark is out with my cousin Nicky this evening. I gave them both my blessing."

Renny eyed her suspiciously but didn't answer.

"Maybe he doesn't want you to know he refused my call. Does the man tell you everything?"

Renny had no time to answer. Her cell phone rang and she picked up quickly when she saw the number. "What's up?—What? No! I'll be right there."

Renny started to run out the door.

"Wait," Sarah forestalled her. "What's happened? Who was that? Where are you headed?"

"It's Julian!" Renny screamed as she ran down the stairs. "There's been an accident. He's at the emergency center at Bellevue..."

Renny kept on mumbling something, but Sarah missed it. She was already out the door.

For a moment Sarah's heart was pounding so hard, the buzzing sound in her ears so loud, she thought she would faint. Inhaling deeply, she schooled herself to calmness. Collecting enough of her thoughts to scavenge through her purse, she looked for Jeff's business card he had handed her once. She dialed him frantically.

"Jeff, are you working right now? I'm sorry, it's Sarah, Sarah Miller."

"Good evening, Sarah Miller. Yes, I have a passenger that I'm dropping off in five minutes. Do you want I go get you?"

"Please, Jeff. And hurry, it's very important."

Sarah asked Jeff to take her to Bellevue, and when he asked which center, she didn't know. "The emergency or the trauma center perhaps. Would you have Miss Renny's cell phone number? She knows."

"Miss Renny gone to First Avenue," Jeff answered with a smile. "She wanted me to take her there, but I already had passenger."

All the way to the hospital Sarah envisaged the worst. She could not believe that the man she loved was in danger of losing his life—this before she would have time to tell him how much she loved him. If anything were to happen to Julian...

Sarah bit her lip and tried to stop the tears, but they still came, pouring out of her in torrents. She dabbed at her eyes with a tissue and desperately tried to muffle her hiccups. Julian was her life. She had always suspected it, even when she despised him. But now she knew it, without the smallest shadow of uncertainty. Just imagining a life without him made her feel small and lost. The deafening thought silenced all possibility of music and joy within her.

Jeff doubled parked in front of the hospital and lunged to open her door. He refused to be paid and looked so forlorn to see her crying that he offered to park properly and go with her.

Sarah thanked him and told him she would be fine.

Just the same, Jeff said he would wait for her.

Inside the entrance hall, a guard gave her directions to the emergency center and Sarah ran down the wide corridors to the two glass doors he had pointed out to her. Inside, a round wooded cubicle served as an admissions' station with several nurses sitting behind the reception alcove.

"Excuse me," she asked in a teary voice, "a Julian Spinner has just been admitted here. I'd like to see him."

The nurse checked her chart. "There is no one by that name that's been admitted here, miss. If there was, they wouldn't be able to receive visitors—unless you're family." The nurse smiled kindly, taking in Sarah's reddened eyes.

Sarah thanked her, then searched the area around her. Down one corridor to her right, she spotted Renny. She was easy to see, all dressed in black against the hospital's white walls. "Renny," she called out and the tall girl walked her way.

"What are you doin' here?" Renny asked, surprised to see her.

"You said Julian…" Sarah stopped talking for fear the water-works would flow again.

Renny guessed at the tragedy behind those few words and took the extra steps to scoop Sarah into her arms. "I'm so sorry, beauty. You asked me who was on the phone. I told you Julian. There's been an accident, but not to Julie. No. They found old Arty near a dumpster. He collapsed from a heart attack."

Sarah disengaged herself from Renny's arms. Her first feeling was immense relief. Julian was fine. He was not hurt. The quick thumping of anticipation of being in his arms again was back with renewed ardor. Then arose the foolish sensation of having run there on so little information.

"Who's Arty?"

Renny looked around at the one nurse still at the station. "Wait until Florence Nightingale here disappears somewhere. Then I'll bring you to the room." Meanwhile, she edged Sarah further down the corridor, quietly, stealthily, cautioning her to be silent. Once they had cleared the back of the desk, she sat down with her on one of the chairs outside a little cubicle closed off by a drawn curtain.

"Arty is an old man who lives on the street. He saved Julie's life—and mine, I'm sure. Julie never told you this?"

Sarah shook her head, more and more curious.

"Julie's old man threw him out of the house one winter. He already had a record at Juvey Hall. I think he was fourteen or somethin'. Anyway, he would have died for sure. No food, no money, no friends to speak of because everyone he hung with was a bum. His mother was furious, but she couldn't do anything."

"That's how he hooked up with Arty?"

"Yeah! Arty gave him a place to live—broken down old warehouse, some cash, some clothes. Then he hooked up with me one day. I'd been on the street since I was ten. I could take care of myself. But Julian was fun. He had all these ideas. Before you knew it, we had ourselves a loyal gang, you know."

Sarah looked at Renny's expression, the dreamy look in her eyes. "You two were lovers, weren't you?"

Renny glanced at her and smiled. "Two decades ago…

that's almost another lifetime. Julie didn't stay long on the street. His father left and he had to go back home to help his mother and his kid brother. When he was there, though, he made all these contacts and stirred up all kinds of loyalties. He used them contacts to make a different life for himself and his family."

"You didn't want to go with him?"

"Julie wanted me to. Back then, we were closer than fuckin' twins." Renny glanced at Sarah. "Sorry for the swear word. I'm gettin' better. I'm takin' speech classes in the city twice a week. Anyway, we was always screwed together tight."

"What happened?" Sarah asked, swallowing the sour bile the picture of Julian with another woman conjured up.

"I couldn't adapt. His mother didn't like me. We were just kids then. It couldn't last. Instead, I concentrated on gettin' through high school—had never even finished grade school. I started workin' out and takin' karate."

Sarah couldn't help thinking that somewhere, Renny was still in love with Julian. She was sure protective of him and his feelings.

"Anyway, Arty is my friend too. They won't let me see him. Julian's there with him. He told 'em he was family."

"Julian's here? Where?" Sarah was determined to see him and speak to him. She had almost lost the chance once; she was not going to waste another minute.

"He won't want to see you, beauty. He doesn't allow

anyone to see him cry. Not even you, the love of his life. Trust me on that one. I'm out here 'cause the big lug won't let me in."

"Please, Renny. I have to see him. I can't wait anymore."

Renny glanced toward the desk. The nurse was gone. "Yeah, I guess it's for a good cause. Listen, I'm sorry if I yelled at you before. Don't be mad at me or anything."

Sarah shook her head and took Renny's hands. "You still care about him a lot, don't you?"

"What do you think? He's my hero. I'll get myself another man some day—when I go lookin', but I only get one hero for the rest of my life. It's a rule," she smiled. "Only one allowed per lifetime."

Sarah agreed, biting her lower lip not to cry.

"You make sure you make him your hero—and never let go. Julie'll love you forever." Renny took Sarah by the arm. "Walk fast and stay right behind me," she urged.

Sarah followed her instructions, literally shadowing the tall girl as Renny took her past the front desk again, then down a corridor to their left. Depressing a green button to one side of a glass door, Renny walked through, snatching Sarah by the arm as she did. "This is how the nurse opened this door before," Renny whispered. "See that blue curtain down there on your right?"

"Yes."

"That's where Arty's stretched out. Julie's there. Just...

don't let him scare you away—Julie, I mean. He can be rough around the edges."

Sarah nodded and gave her a little squeeze. She tiptoed the two hundred feet to the designated curtain. When she turned to check for Renny, the tall girl had gone.

Taking a deep breath, she walked in. It took a few minutes for her eyes to adjust to the dimness of the small room loaded with pristine gleaming metal equipment.

On the farthest wall was a stretcher, covered with a white sheet outlining the contours of a person. Sarah glimpsed Julian standing with his back to her, staring down at the man beside him. Sarah realized that no one had heard her enter. She cleared her throat to let Julian know she was there.

"I'm going to stay a while longer, nurse," he simply said without looking at her. "He's not showing any signs of recovery."

"I'm sorry to hear that, Julian."

He didn't budge, but she saw his back stiffen. Instead, he half-turned, gave her a sidelong glance and asked her nonplus. "What the hell are you doing here?"

Sarah suddenly realized how strange her presence there had to appear to Julian. She had not shown him any signs of life all this time, and here she was at the hospital partaking of his private personal moment with this man, this part of his life he had never even mentioned to her.

All at once she was wishing she were somewhere else. "I heard from Renny that you were at the hospital—the emergency...I mistook her information...thought you were hurt."

"Well, now you see that I'm not, please leave."

"Look, I know I deserve your scorn. But the least you can do is hear me out before you decide to cut me out of your life for good. I mean, you wouldn't take my phone call..."

"When?"

"Earlier this evening. I told the sitter my name. She came back..."

"That was you?" He said breathless.

"Yes."

"She doesn't speak much English. She told me it was the nice young girl who stayed at the house. Lately this reporter, Raines, has been camping out on our doorstep. She's working on a project with Mark. I thought that's whom she meant." Julian put his face in his hands, trying to rub the fatigue away.

"So the dinner engagement..." Sarah asked tentatively.

He turned to look at her, and Sarah's heart sank as she saw, even in the dark, how tired and haggard his eyes were. There were no dancing lights in the twin grey pools, no cocky smile on his full lips. Just a tired, drawn expression with what resembled a two-day growth of beard on his cheeks.

"I had dinner with Melissa—in the dining room. A formal affair with candles."

"How thoughtful of you," Sarah told him, barely holding back the urge to run into his arms. She would beg if need be. He had to love her again. He just had to.

"I was offering her an olive branch instead of being able to fulfill my promise to her."

"What promise?" Sarah asked softly.

"To find a wife, so she can have a mother."

Without realizing it, Sarah had started taking small steps toward him, attracted to him like a featherweight to a giant magnet. "There are many women who would love to be your wife, Julian," she told him in a soft voice.

"There is only one that I want. And she's made it clear that she does not want me."

As she got closer, she noticed how red and swollen his eyes were. She extended a hand to smooth his brow. It was damp and furrowed. "I'm sorry about your friend, Julian," she told him in a fractured voice.

"So am I. But he's not the reason...my eyes...look tired," he told her, his voice low and rough.

Sarah shivered and all the words she had wanted to say to him jammed in a mind that spun like a wheel. Faced with his pain, the only words she could find to utter made no sense. "You've been crying, Julian. There's no shame in that. You can say it, you know." She looked at the man on the stretcher, the heart monitor ticking away, artificial life flowing in and out of his body. And when she stepped into Julian's eyes, although her craving to be in his arms was so intense she could hardly breathe, she knew she would have to wait.

"You're right," he exhaled, having come closer. "There

is no shame in crying. Not when it burns so much, so hard, you can no longer stand the ache. It's actually a form of release—of letting go. It purges the heart so that one day it may love again."

Sarah gazed into those tender eyes. Thank god, they were at odds with his words. She could not believe that all he needed was to cry to be done with her.

Then she remembered her own swollen red eyes. "For some of us, crying is another form of release—a beautiful revelation of emotions that were hidden away…or tossed aside out of fear. That's why I cried, Julian."

He smiled and nodded, but said nothing.

"I know this is not the time or the place. But, I called you earlier because I wanted us to have a chat. Can we still do that? Will you listen to what I have to say?"

"I will listen, Sarah."

She found him extremely non-committal, aloof even. She wondered yet again if it was too late, at the same time questioning a man's feelings that would fizzle so quickly.

CHAPTER THIRTEEN

Arty passed away without fanfare early Tuesday morning. Julian insisted he get a proper burial and be laid to rest on consecrated grounds. He had been born a Catholic, Arty had told him, on the north side of Belfast. There was no knowledge of family, but the small Catholic Church in Brooklyn filled quickly with a strange mixture of mourners. There were hobos and the less fortunate, a few guests in limos with entourages, and of course, Julian and his family and the friends who knew what Arty had meant to him.

There had been no chance for Sarah to talk to Julian. She had immersed herself in her music, fearful of calling his place at the wrong time.

And as she followed the silent funeral cortege, shouldered by Nicky and Mark, she kept an eye out for Julian, one of the pallbearers.

They waited for the limo to leave then filed into Julian's jeep. Mark drove with Nicky beside him, while Sarah, Bella and Frank piled into the back. Julian rode in the hearse.

No one said a word, each person lost in his own thoughts. Even Nicky was blankly staring out the window and Sarah could not help wondering if she and Mark had hit it off. Nicky had never said. There had been so little time for conversations, as far as she knew they had only had the one date.

The reception was muted and eerie. It was served at a nearby restaurant, and three small taxi vans had shuttled those unable to get there under their own steam. The buffet was diverse and opulent.

Sarah was surprised at how Julian had thought of every little detail. She wondered if he had had assistance with the preparation, and if he was the kind to welcome help in such a situation. How would she fit into the life of this formidable man who oversaw his family and friends as a pastor tends his flock? Deep in contemplation, arranging an array of vegetables on her plate, she did not notice the tall man who slid up behind her.

Julian took a long whiff of her scented hair and, so as not to startle her, reached with his hand beside hers to gather some vegetables from the tray.

As soon as Sarah noticed the hand she recognized it, the long fingers and the large wrists. She strove to remain outwardly calm, even though her heart was drumming its own wild song inside her chest.

"Thank you for coming," he whispered softly against her temple.

She closed her eyes, relishing the flutter of emotions welling up inside her. "It was the least I could do," she answered pleasantly. "It must have taken a lot of effort and a few heads to plan this. Or did you do it yourself?"

She turned to look at him, and his tentative smile as well as the question in his dark eyes indicated he was not quite sure where she was headed with this.

"I did have help," he answered tentatively. "Your cousin Nicky had some good ideas, as did Mark."

"I'm glad," she smiled. I'm especially glad that you now know there was no reason for you to be…so…enraged with me last Sunday evening."

He lost his smile and his face grew stern. For the first time, Sarah saw him at a loss for words. They both knew that he had spent far too much time agonizing over her date with Mark, agonizing for nothing—to the point of driving himself insanely jealous.

"I would appreciate it if you never mentioned that episode again, Sarah," he asked her more than demanded. "In my life, I've cried twice. Even on those two occasions, no one was ever aware of it."

She gave him a teasing smile. "When?"

"I'm entrusting you with my most precious secret," he told her, flicking the tip of her nose. "At the birth of Melissa," he stared into her eyes. "And when Brad was born. I guess I'm a sentimental fool when it comes to births."

She nodded, taking in the meaning of his words. "This means your crying days are far from over."

He lost his smile. A small muscle twitched in his lower jaw and the onyx eyes darkened dangerously. "How about that chat you promised me?" he breathed.

"I've been waiting," she taunted him, "waiting for you to have time for me." She smiled at the tremor on his face.

"I can't believe you just said that." He relaxed, knowing she was teasing. "I almost called you fifty times this week. Every time I was faced with a flower arrangement, or a guest I couldn't find, or the menu for this damn buffet." He closed his eyes. "I would have loved to consult with you on this project, given you the reins…"

"Why didn't you?"

"There was always someone around who knew better. Mark said it was not fair to burden you with this. Renny insisted we sit down and work through our issues before I ask for your help. Jessica Raines laughed when I proposed calling you."

"You listen to Jessica Raines?"

"Not anymore. She knew how to push my buttons, Sarah. Not the ones she wanted, obviously," he smiled. "She put me through hell with her little announcement one Friday afternoon."

"I thought she might have had a hand in it. I should

have called you first, Julian. It's just that...I was finally so clear on my intentions it never dawned on me that you would think otherwise."

He took the plate from her hands and put it down next to his. "Are you very hungry?" he asked her without a smile, eyes smoldering.

She closed her eyes and nodded. When she opened them, his face mirrored deep disappointment.

"Really?" he asked with a frown.

She stroked his cheek. "I'm sure we can find some other form of nourishment to curb my appetite." She smiled up at him.

"Don't tease, Sarah. No more playing with my heart. We have a lot of talking and explaining to do before there can ever be sex between us—I think you know that."

"I do," she continued, unrelenting, the smile deepening. "But I told you once before, Julian. I am not a tease. I don't like empty words or empty promises. And I'm not going to run and hide anymore. Now...can we have sex?"

"You little witch," he laughed. "I mean it, Sarah. I want answers. I want to know everything there is to know about you—no more surprises. I want to share who I am with you—no holding back. I don't care if this takes weeks to do. It's going to happen before I lift another finger to touch you."

"We had best get started then," she answered playfully.

He placed an arm around her shoulders and walked

with her to where her brother and Nicky were standing. Renny was talking to Bella, and Jeff was stacking another plateful of pasta and cheese. All of them stopped what they were doing to watch the two of them happily sauntering down the restaurant aisle. Bella had tears in her eyes and Nicky was jubilant.

Mark winked at Sarah. "Nice to see you found the courage," he whispered as she came close to him.

"I'm leaving you in charge, Mark. And I'm taking your car." Julian turned toward Sarah. "We are leaving. We'll see you all later."

Sarah acknowledged with a bright smile.

Outside in the car, Julian revved the motor and lowered the top.

The wind was invigorating and soothing. The morning had been so warm and it wasn't getting any cooler, Sarah thought, not with Julian Spinner's virile presence beside her to heat things up. Unlike the jeep, the car was close quarters. Their shoulders were constantly touching and rubbing due to Julian's need to shift. Sarah eyed Julian's right hand on the stick shift more than once. Each time she did, she shivered at the sight of his wide hand forcefully directing the stick, claiming it as he rested on it, his fingers long and firmly spread around it. She could not help remembering how gentle and agile those hands had been when they had made love to her.

Julian pulled the car up in front of her apartment. He waited for the occupant in front of him to leave before squeezing into his spot. "Now I know why you don't keep a car in the city. Is this all the parking there is?"

"There's a garage at the back, but it's always full." Sarah straightened and had to ask, "I thought we were headed to Long Island?"

"You weren't paying attention," Julian smiled. "I thought it might be smart for you to collect a few of your things before heading east—bathing suit, a small suitcase. By the looks of things, we're going to have a lot to discuss—don't you think?"

She nodded. As she made to exit, she noticed the top was still down, the motor still running and Julian wasn't budging. "Aren't you coming in?"

"If it's okay, Sarah, I'll wait for you here."

"Well, it's not okay. It would be nice to have a little help, a cup of coffee. I have strawberries in the refrigerator that will go to waste." Sarah checked his face. He was staring in front of him, mutinous and determined. "And I haven't eaten this morning."

He turned in his seat just enough to glance at her upturned, expectant face and smiled. "Tell you what. Grab what you need, and we'll stop off at the restaurant of your choice to have anything you want."

She knew what she wanted and it had nothing to do with food—restaurant or otherwise. "I don't understand… Why the fuss? You've helped me gather my things before—remember? What's the difference?"

Julian gave her a knowing look, stopped the engine and turned to face her.

"There is a huge difference. You were so scared of me I didn't dare move right or left for fear you'd cry rape. I just couldn't wait to get out of there—even when you took your sweet time."

"So? Nothing's changed."

He nodded and gave her a wry smile. "For one thing, you're no longer scared of me. You own me now, don't you?"

Sarah lowered her eyes and bit her bottom lip not to smile. She did not own him at this precise minute, but she intended to—sooner than he expected.

He extended an arm to gently run his fingers through her hair, undoing her ponytail. "Sarah, you of all people know I can't go up there with you." His voice was soft and his eyes kind. He planted a kiss on the top of her head as he continued to smooth her hair. "If I go up there with you, sweetie, once that door closes behind us…you know," he moaned. "Do I have to spell it out?"

He leaned his forehead against her temple and Sarah could feel his warm breath on her cheek. "Would that be so bad?" she whispered softly.

He backed up to look into her eyes. "Yes it would be. I told you, there's a lot we have to discuss. I'm still not clear on your feelings for me, on whether I've bullied you into caring for me."

"That's ridiculous!" she exclaimed.

"Is it? You'd never been with anybody before, Sarah. And because of this hunger...this need I have for you, I almost lost you."

He bent and kissed her temple. "I traumatized you and scared you senseless." His voice was a mere raspy whisper. "I want to be in bed with you so much it chokes me; I can't think straight, I can't sleep, anything I eat tastes the same..."

Sarah took a deep breath. "Who are you to say if I'm ready or not?"

For a long minute they just stared at each other, Sarah's eyes showing desire and willingness, Julian's eyes loving and determined to stand pat.

"Okay." She took a deep breath. "It's true. When I met you, I had the emotional awareness of a fourteen year old. And that may be stretching it a bit." She smiled. "I was raised in a gilded cage. I didn't grow up going to movies or socializing with young people my own age until I came here to America. And that was to study. I had this image of a prince charming—who would sweep me off my feet." Sarah wiped a tear. It was difficult for her to put this into exact words, especially with Julian looking on so intensely. "At first, my prince charming looked a lot like Mark." She spoke hesitantly, seeing the shadow cross his eyes. "He was compatible. We shared so many common things. He was dashing and kind...easy to be with—mostly non-threatening, or at least nothing I couldn't handle." She placed a hand on his resting in his lap. "I have you to thank, Julian. Loving Mark would have been the biggest mistake of my life. It would have taken me…weeks, months…who knows how long…who cares, to discover that my soul mate was not the person I most tended to laugh with, shared commonalities with, or liked to befriend. My soul mate is the one person I can touch and feel instantly energized, finally replete after years of solitude; the one pair of eyes who can mirror who I am, the same eyes who can see the reflection of who he could be and all that he is in mine."

Sarah saw Julian close his eyes and lean his head against the window. Slowly he took a ragged breath. When she saw that he was relishing the moment and not looking at her she tugged at his thigh. "Julian?"

He grabbed her hand to steady it, and he stared at her with glistening eyes.

"I may be immature, but I'm not a child. And I know without the slightest doubt…that I love you. I am head-over-heels, forget-to-eat, can't-get-to-sleep, madly in love with you. I love you, Julian. I want it to be forever…"

"Stop!" He took deep breaths to calm down. "It's too soon, Sarah. This is exactly what I wanted to avoid. I want us to share what you shared with Mark—I was so jealous of your outings with the children, your camaraderie whenever your laughter resonated throughout the house. I need your friendship, your respect. I need your kindness—I want you to like me."

"I think I understand," she smiled.

"Sarah, I feel so privileged that you think me your soul mate. Will you also be my friend?"

She nodded, impressed and delighted that he intended to be such a big part of her life. Boldly she moved closer toward him. There was nowhere for him to retreat; he was already fully leaning against his door. "As my new friend's first duty, would you help me out with something?"

He gave her a quizzical glance, his jittery nerves wondering where she was headed. "Anything within reason," he said cautiously.

"You once told me you give karate lessons, right?"

He nodded, relieved they were changing the subject. "People say I am a good instructor. I can teach you if you like." He was pleased she was taking steps toward that friendship he had mentioned.

"I am counting on it—you teaching me, I mean." She let her wide eyes travel from his furrowed brow to the quizzical look in his eyes, to his lips parted with surprise, to the little pulse beating on the side of his neck. "I need you to teach me how to make love," she added softly.

Sarah saw him physically recoil as if struck by a jolt, a low blow hitting him hard below the belt. He had no words, but she could tell he was holding his breath. "That's good," she whispered. "You would need to stay exactly still, as you are now—not move or budge, and instruct me on how to touch you properly." She slipped a finger between his lips, tugging on the bottom one to make it drop. Delicately she slid the tip of her tongue inside the small opening, brushing up against his. She heard him groan. But still he did not budge.

She pulled away and smiled. "See, I knew you would be strong enough to do it. You'll need to tell me where to kiss you," she whispered, applying her tongue to the lobe of his ear. "Or would you rather it deeper?" She moved her tongue inside his ear. "You'll have to teach me how to best caress you, fondle you; how to pull and tug," she continued, jerking his chin gently while her eyes smiled into his. "I am an excellent student, my love. I will practice and practice until I get it perfectly right," she purred, trailing her fingers down his head to the base of his neck, delicately rubbing her breasts against his chest.

No longer able to resist, he grabbed her by the shoulders, squeezing her hard and pushed her away from him. Looking deep into her eyes, he nodded, surreptitiously at first, then more vigorously as he saw the pleasure in her eyes deepen at his capitulation. "I told you. You own me."

Faced with the raw pleasure on her face, he closed his eyes and moaned. Then he shook his head, a wry half-smile flitting on his face like a white flag. Silently he turned the key to put up the top to the convertible. He alighted from the car, crossed to Sarah's side to open her door and help her out.

Face to face with the woman he loved, he bent his head and kissed her gently on the mouth, his tongue throbbing against hers. "First lesson," he told her roughly as he took her by the hand to lead the way, "I like your whole tongue in my mouth when you kiss me, not just the tip of it."

Sarah acknowledged with a nod and a smile, holding his arm firmly for support. One thing she knew with joyful certainty, she would perform exactly as instructed with the greatest of pleasure.

Sarah was the first to wake up the next morning. The sun was already high and she suspected it was late. When she glanced at her watch, she read 9:00 on the dial. She was glad she had warned her group the day before that she would be absent today.

She stretched and smiled when she felt Julian lying beside her. Propped up on an elbow against her pillow, she watched him sleep. He was lying on his back, oblivious to everything and everyone around him. So much for heightened senses, she smiled, caressing him with her eyes.

It's no wonder he lay spent and exhausted; they had only fallen asleep a couple of hours before, it seemed. They had made love during that afternoon, talked all evening, and while promising one another they would sleep in each other's arms the whole night through, they had ended up riveted together tighter than a nut and bolt, writhing with desire until the early hours of the morning.

Sarah pulled up the tangled sheet piled at his feet to cover him, thinking he might like to sleep a little longer. He sure deserved it.

Delicately, she donned her robe that was folded at the

foot of the bed, and stepped down to go to the bathroom. On her way back, the telephone rang and startled her. She picked up as fast as she could not wanting it to wake Julian.

"Hello?" she whispered.

It was Nicky. She sounded excited. "So? Did he ask you yet? We're all holed up at the Long Island casa dying to hear. We figured you two officially became a couple yesterday—when you didn't show up for dinner."

"Ask me what?" She barely had time to finish her question before Julian stretched over and took the phone from her.

"Nicky, now's not the time. Sarah will call you later." Gently, Julian replaced the receiver and smiled at Sarah, his eyes closely examining her reaction.

There was puzzlement in Sarah's eyes, and a peevish hint about her mouth that did not bode well. *He can't just arbitrarily decide to end my calls for me.*

He heaved a weary loaded sigh and plopped back down in bed. "I apologize for that…" He indicated the phone. "Don't worry; I'm not usually such a creep…It's just that I've been lying in bed here for the past hour…" He looked at her, noticing her features had softened though questions still lined her forehead.

"And I thought you were sleeping," she said softly as she sat on the bed. Shyly, she began caressing his head sensuously with the tips of her fingers, trying to encourage him to continue. "I know that Nicky had no business calling this early in the morning. She just worries about me."

"You can say that again." He reached for the hand that was driving him crazy, kissed it as he arrested it. "I'm still of the same mind I was yesterday, though, Sarah. I don't want to corner you or pressure you in any way. Nicky and the others...they think I should...ask you to...well, make my intentions clear—for the future..." He sighed, realizing he was stumbling over his feelings, worried she would say no and he would lose her, worried she would say yes and he would lose her later. "I guess you know what I mean."

She nodded, tears in her eyes. She bent and kissed his lips, tugging on them with her teeth, relishing them with her tongue. "Don't you know by now how much I completely and totally belong to you? How much I love you?"

He nodded, returning her kiss. "I don't doubt it anymore—not like I did yesterday." He turned to better see her, poised over him like a guardian angel. He caressed her face, her neck, and toyed with the strands of her hair tickling his chest. "You're going to be one hell of a rich lady in a couple of weeks. Have you thought about that?"

She nodded, her eyes not straying from his.

"And you're one fine cello player—going to be famous—hell, you already are. Have you also thought about that?"

She smiled and nodded again, her eyes deeply lodged in his.

"So, what do you have to say for yourself?" he asked unceremoniously.

"I don't want to disappoint you, my love, but in a couple of weeks we are going to be a hell of a rich couple." She smiled from ear to ear, kissing the tip of his nose. "And as for me being a famous cellist, I don't mind having an adoring audience of one."

He snorted. "Be serious. Don't dodge these questions, sweetheart," he told her as he flipped her underneath him, kissing the will out of her while relishing her soft moans.

When he allowed her to breathe again, she asked him in a low husky tone, "Isn't this answer enough?"

He shook his head, the hint of a shadow in his eyes. "To a proud man like me, being hitched to a famous rich beauty like yourself will be difficult, Sarah. I need some sort of reassurance."

She caressed his cheek. "I'd be the last person in the world to reassure you. I'm just getting acquainted with my own heart, Julian…"

He pulled away, her words only confirming his reason to worry even more.

"But what I do know," she forestalled his next words with a finger across his lips, "is that when I thought you were hovering between life and death in the hospital, I felt as if someone had robbed me of all my joy. All the music that normally spins 'round in my head was suddenly silent. There was no reason to go on enjoying my life. No reason to smile, to feel the sun on my face. That's when I realized that the music, the money…none of it mattered if I couldn't share it with you."

He nodded, somewhat appeased. "You're still so young, Sarah."

She stared at him in wonderment. "You, the progressive father that has his daughter study way beyond her years...you're not afraid she'll turn out smarter than you are, are you?"

"It's not the same thing."

"It is if you're trying to act as my father and decide what's good and what's not so good for me." Sarah's gaze did not budge. She waited for him to understand, to realize that she was wise enough and intelligent enough to make this leap with him.

Her eyes held him captive until he could bear it no more and had to bend to seal their lips in a passionate kiss.

His cell phone rang, interrupting their bliss.

"May I?" he labored to ask, their breath still mingling. "It might be Ray." When she motioned to go ahead he turned, stretching to reach the phone in his coat pocket draped over the chair beside the bed.

"Yeah, I hear you."

Sarah waited patiently, sitting up and nestling her head in the crux of his arm.

Julian was shaking his head, trying to hear. "There's a lot of static in the background...can you hear me? Yes, she's here with me." After a couple of tense seconds Julian lost the connection. "The phone's dead." He threw it back in his jacket pocket. "Renny's policing the area, making certain I'm in the right place with the right person." He smiled.

"What did she want?"

Julian shrugged, his mood buoyed by the memory of the very last comment she had served him before he had lost his head and kissed her. "Just something she is trying to locate for me. I'll need to call her later to get the details."

Sarah sobered somewhat, realizing he still had his little secrets. But it was the first phone call—the one from Nicky—that had caught her attention and that was still foremost on her mind. She wondered if her youth, her music and her money were just convenient excuses for him to waylay any commitment toward fashioning a relationship with her. The last thing in the world she wanted to do was to trap him into a hasty decision.

"What's going on behind those beautiful eyes of yours?" he asked, mystified by her sudden change of mood.

"I wanted to ask you if you would be kind enough to grade my first lesson," she asked demurely. She knew it was a long shot, but she had to draw the point home.

He tilted his head and questioned her with a squint of his eyes.

"How did I score?" She lowered the sheet and rubbed his abdomen. "You know, with my first love-making lesson?"

He groaned and opened her robe, anxious to have her skin rubbing up against his. He lay down on top of her, quickly demonstrating that common sense had left his body. Driving him now was an overwhelming and growing desire to lunge inside her. "You are the quickest study I have ever had the pleasure to teach," he whispered against her mouth. "And the adventure is just beginning, my sweet. There is so much more to explore."

He gave her his most wicked smile, the one that used to scare her so. Now all it did was make her liquid inside, and have her thrust her legs apart obediently, as far as she could. "Now do you think you could teach me about long-term commitment and how to maintain a strong relationship?" she breathed, a soft moan escaping from her as he caressed the insides of her legs.

He laughed against her cheek, a low chuckle, as he realized she was cleverly guiding his thoughts to line up with hers. "Between you and Melissa, I think my goose is cooked," he answered as he unleashed on her mind-numbing pleasures that melted all her resolve.

CHAPTER FOURTEEN

By the time they reached Westbury it was almost one o'clock. Mark had just arrived from picking up Nicky. Frank and Bella had slept at the house, and Brad and Melissa ran out to greet them with screams and giggles.

"Daddy, Daddy!" Brad was jumping up and down. Julian picked him up like the small weight that he was and plopped him on his shoulders.

The gesture had Sarah recall the first time she had seen Julian walking down the laneway with Brad on his back. How confused she had been with her feelings toward this rude man; and now this man was hers, body and soul. She shivered as he held out his hand for her, hooking her tightly as he smiled deep into her eyes.

On her other side, Sarah felt a little hand squeeze hers. She smiled down at Melissa, who gave her a cute little nod and wink. Sarah laughed, touched by the child's acuity, and responded in kind.

It was clear Julian was happy to be home. He loved his children and spending time with them was not always easy. "Okay, guys," he laughed. "On with the suits and everyone into the pool."

The children cheered happily.

Sarah was happy too, because even as the afternoon wore on, the heat never let up. The day continued to be hot and hazy. Frank and Bella both lounged in chairs under the shade trees while the children splashed in the pool under Mark's supervision.

After swimming to her heart's content, Sarah stretched out beside Nicky, trying to catch end of afternoon rays. Nicky had confided that she had seen Mark regularly since that first Sunday, and though they were not yet hot and heavy, their relationship was a promising one.

"I mean, no one's ever going to be hotter than you and Julian. My God, Sarah, the man worships you." Nicky applied more lotion to her fair skin.

"I guess. Although, we've discussed a long-term commitment…I don't think he's quite ready yet."

"He was burned with his first wife, don't forget. Probably just wants to make sure you two mesh well, before…'I do,' you know."

Sarah shook her head, her sunglasses hiding her eyes. "I don't know. I think it's more than that."

Julian had left them a couple of hours ago. He had said he had business to tend to with his attorneys. He had not specified and Sarah had not asked for details. She hoped he would be forthcoming with them eventually.

"Speak of the devil," whispered Nicky. "Look who is standing by the deck over there, looking tall and sexy."

Sarah lifted her head and noticed Julian talking with Frank and Bella. He wore loose cotton pants and a long sleeveless T-shirt tucked in at the waist.

"I never told you this, Sarah. But that day I went to see Julian at the gym, I almost ran out of there without saying a word to him. He scared the wits out of me."

Sarah laughed at her a little. "Serves you right for meddling."

"No. I mean he glued me to the spot with his…maleness, and he put me through such a flux of strange feelings, I thought, one day I would tell you just how formidable this man really is. You did some job resisting him for so long."

"Thank you—I think." Sarah was happy just to lie there, exhausted and enormously relaxed.

"Here he comes," shot Nicky, the little drama in her voice meant to amuse.

Sarah raised the back of her chair and watched him walk across the lawn toward her. He was gorgeous, she thought, her heart thumping away.

"Come," he said peremptorily as he approached her. "I'm taking you away from all this."

Sarah was about to flick him a hand salute, so bossy did he sound; but she saw the wicked smile playing on his lips and knew he was teasing her.

"Me, too?" Nicky whined, taking her turn to make fun.

"Just Sarah," Julian answered, still staring at her.

A decided edge to his tone forced her to search his eyes. All she saw in them was rock-hard determination and she wondered about some problem. She tied a summer shawl around her waist and walked with him to the house.

"Did I ever tell you how beautiful you look in a bikini?"

"I guess there'll be many firsts in both our lives. We're just getting to know each other," she smiled.

He frowned. "You don't have regrets already, do you?"

"Silly," she elbowed him. "I just hope there's room for me in your busy schedule, Julian."

"Look who's talking!" he exclaimed.

"No, I mean it. You've been used to doing everything on your own for so long. It's a hard habit to break." She was thinking about his afternoon escapade and was wondering if he was ever going to tell her about it without her having to inquire.

He drew her into his arms. "I've wanted to do this all afternoon," he nuzzled her, his heart beating fast. "Come, he coaxed her."

As Julian and Sarah climbed up to the deck, Bella got

up to give Sarah a huge hug as she was passing by. "You're such a lovely girl—to take care of our Julian," she cooed with a low throttle of a laugh.

As for Frank, he looked at Sarah and winked, smiling his approval of her and Julian together. "You two make a handsome couple. There'll be more good looking children running around these lawns."

Sarah smiled and stared at Julian. What had he been telling them—children?

"I told Frank and Bella that we had decided to date—formally, right?" He asked her to corroborate.

She nodded, albeit disappointingly. "Right," she answered, glad at least he was not being close-mouthed about their relationship. She would have hated to sneak around his friends and family with him.

Officially, Sarah had unpacked her things in the guest bedroom, the one that communicated with Julian's room. Now that she was on the premises, she was not quite sure how this would work. He had told his aunt and uncle about them, Mark and Nicky already knew, as did Renny. Did this mean they could officially share a room? She checked the communicating door as she changed from her suit to a summer dress. He was there, since he had just come up with her. He made no motion to enter or even knock. Would he simply ignore her now that she was here? Ignore her and go about his business?

Ten minutes later, Julian knocked on the door between

their rooms. "May I come in?"

Sarah ran to the door. She had forgotten the latch. "It was locked from before," she tried to explain apologetically.

"That's okay, sweetheart." He took her hand and waited, as if needing permission before invading her space. "You look beautiful, Sarah."

She smiled, still a little intimidated by him. "You look handsome too." She surveyed his shirt and Bermuda kakis.

"Bar-B-Q wear, you think?"

She nodded, covered the distance between them and softly kissed his cheek. She felt him tremble as he clutched her in his arms, crushing her against him.

"Come," he told her once he had regained some composure. He walked with her to the window seat that overlooked the front gardens. "Sit with me," he smiled. "I think we need to talk," he explained to relieve the surprise on her face. "Just a minute," he urged her. Then he strode to the communicating door, closed it and locked it. He came back to her a wicked light in his eyes. "Don't look so worried. I'm not going to ravish you…" He laughed at her a little. "Although I might, if you give me permission." He sat with her, taking both her hands. "I'm afraid I haven't taught my children the proper decorum for entering their parents' room. Being a single father, I let that slip. They're liable to come in without knocking any time they know I'm home and out of view."

"That's why you carried me back that first morning."

He nodded. "What's worse, they're early risers." He

stared out the window for a long time. Then he searched her eyes. "I should have asked you to come with me this afternoon. I'm sorry I kept it such a secret. It's just something that happened before you and I became…a couple," he stroked her cheek. "Even when I drove you home yesterday, after the funeral…I had no idea, Sarah, that we would even become an official couple so soon."

"That's my fault, Julian, I'm sorry."

"It's not a fault, and I hope you're not sorry!" he exclaimed.

"I have no regrets," she argued, "just sorry that you feel you were rushed."

"That's not what concerns me," he added softly. "I had planned weeks—months—of courtship; getting to know each other, liking each other. I wanted to do it right this time." He hesitated. "I married Marissa because she was pregnant, Sarah. I'd been with her once. We didn't love each other. We just wanted to make a home for the baby she was carrying—our child."

"Mark said you were madly in love with her…"

He laughed. "Our Mark, he has a flare for the dramatics. Did he also give you his ridiculous rendition of how my big klutzy fingers fumble over the oboe?"

Sarah laughed spontaneously. "He did! How did you know?"

"He must have viewed me as a threat early on." Julian shook his head. "I use the routine to amuse the children sometimes. Melissa plays the oboe—like an angel. I play the piano, Sarah. I'm just an amateur, mind you. But I like to play now and then."

"That's wonderful," she smiled with a tease in her voice. "We can play a duet sometime. You can tickle the ivories, while I pluck at the strings…" She presented him with her lips.

"Stop that, Sarah. You sure know how to push my buttons." He heaved a heavy sigh.

"I'm sorry," she laughed, making light of his predicament. "Anyway, you're right about Mark. I think he did suspect early on. Probably saw our future—yours and mine—in my eyes."

He lost his smile and his eyes became darker. "Did he—do you? Do you see a long-term future for us, Sarah?"

If someone had pricked a needle in her joyfully puffed-up heart, Sarah would not have been more devastated. "Julian," she breathed, "I may not be as worldly or…or as experienced as you are in a lot of things. But what I said to you yesterday, I meant. I admit, I…I may be a bit of a dunce where heart matters are concerned. And I took a long time to come around. But that's only because I needed to be sure—doubly sure…" Sarah noticed his eyes were still questioning slits. "Is this because I didn't meet your…needs…? I can learn to do better over time…"

"Oh, God, Sarah!" He bent to stroke her temple with his mouth. "Don't ever, ever think that. You were amazing. Do you know the talent it takes to have a man love you for hours at a time?" He kissed her ear as she shook her head. "Ask your friend Nicky. Ask Renny. Ask them how long it lasts."

"Doesn't that depend on the man?" she whispered, nuzzling him back.

He groaned softly. "It takes two to dance, my sweet." Tearing himself away, he looked into her eyes. "I'm ten years older than you are. I have two children…"

"I like your children, Julian—a lot. And I think they like me…"

He shook his head. "They love you, Sarah, especially Melissa."

"Then don't make this about the children, or your age, or the fact that I'm inexperienced or that we had such a rocky start…"

"That was my next objection…"

"This is about you, Julian. About the fact that you're not ready to commit to our official status of…whatever that may be. And you don't need to explain. There aren't any plausible reasons to validate insecurity. I know. I've just spent six weeks struggling with mine. It doesn't matter whether it's because you were burned or simply that you are taking a wait-and-see attitude." She smiled and stroked his cheek. "I'm going to be right here. I'm not going anywhere. Oh! I have to go to France in less than three weeks—but that's another story," she smiled, trying to relieve some of the instant disappointment in his eyes.

He rose, taking a few steps away from her, staring out the window. "I don't mind telling you, I'm surprised."

She saw by the look on his face that he was serious.

"I'd hoped that you were going to fight for that official status of whatever it is we are…" he continued. "I mean, I've already told my aunt and uncle. While here you are," he stared at her upturned face, "looking pleased and almost relieved."

She rose and almost lunged at him in protest, scrutinizing his eyes until she saw a small light lurking in the onyx jewels. "You are acting crazy," she said softly. "What's going on?"

He cocked an eyebrow and smiled. "Crazy? I'll have you know I'm certifiable. Sit," he ordered her.

She gave him a defiant smile, but sat anyway.

Julian reached into his pocket and sat back down beside her. He took her hand, turned it face up and deposited a small velvet box into it.

"Julian," she breathed. "What have you done?"

"Open it," he told her roughly.

Inside was the biggest, shiniest princess cut diamond Sarah had ever seen. She could not get her fingers to pluck the ring from the box, she was trembling so hard. She tried to stop the tears from wetting her cheeks, but they would not obey.

"Here," he whispered against her cheek, "let me."

Only then did she realize that he was kneeling beside her. "Sarah, will you be my wife, my life-partner, my love for all time?" he asked as he slipped the ring onto her finger.

She glanced down at his eyes overflowing with love. She closed her own eyes, too overwhelmed to talk and simply nodded as she tried not to let her smile turn into a grimace of tears. She allowed him to place the ring on her finger, and stared dreamily at the large diamond that fit perfectly.

He rose, tugging her up with him and held her until her crying subsided.

"I hadn't realized you love me as much as you do—the way I love you," she finally had the courage to tell him.

He took a tissue from his pocket and handed it to her. "The result of having children around." He nuzzled her hair. "You always have tissues handy."

"Is this what you were really doing this afternoon? Out shopping for a ring?"

He shook his head. "No, I've had this ring for weeks. I bought it the very next Monday after we first slept together."

"Were you already preparing for a repeat performance—in case I was pregnant?"

He laughed loudly. "You may not remember, sweetheart, but I wore protection that night—lots of them. No, this afternoon…" He heard his cell phone ringing in his bedroom. "Excuse me." He ran to answer, while Sarah followed. "Ray? Yes. I hear you. But stop moving. I am losing you." Julian opened his left arm for Sarah to nestle there as he tried to make out what Ray Cox was saying. "You found shed number 9…and…did you look under the bricks? What do you mean shed number 6? There are no bricks in number 9?"

Sarah was staring at him, more and more curious.

"So, old Arty was dyslexic. Who cares? Is it there?" Julian was shaking his head, trying to hear. "There's a lot of static in the background...a mail bag? What's in it?" After a few minutes, Julian smiled from ear to ear. "That crazy old fool. All that money! Who would've thought? Yeah, Ray. Thanks a heap. Can you get it to Sal? Yeah, he's standing by. Talk to you later."

"What was that all about?"

Julian smiled, pleased with himself, with her, with the whole world. "It's what I was arranging this afternoon. The Arty Maiz Foundation for wayward kids. It has a nice ring to it, don't you think? And it's starting off with close to half a million dollars."

"Who is the benefactor—you?"

He smiled. "Arty Maiz, who else?"

When she stared up at him, incredulity stamped in wide green eyes, Julian added, scooping her up with an arm around her waist. "How would you like to hear a story—it dates back a few years and peeks at some of my not-so-nice past, but it ends well. I think you'll enjoy it."

"I'm sure I can suffer through a story with you as the main character," she giggled, as happy as a schoolgirl.

"Come on, let's go show everyone that rock—make it really official."

As he walked through his room toward the door to the

communicating door Sarah had closed, he hesitated. "Let's leave it. The children will have to learn to knock before they enter from now on." He gazed into her eyes. "I'm never sleeping alone again," he whispered inches away from her lips.

"You mean, without me," Sarah smiled as she précised. "I like that version better," she muttered, her tongue already hampered by his.

You can guess the rest...